CALVIN
AND THE
SUGAR
APPLES

CALVIN

AND THE

SUGAR APPLES

INÊS F. OLIVEIRA

ILLUSTRATED BY
VANESSA BALEZZA

THE
collective
BOOK STUDIO

Library of Congress Cataloging-in-Publication Data available.
ISBN: 978-1-68555-219-0
Ebook ISBN: 978-1-68555-070-7
Library of Congress Control Number: 2022916492

Printed using Forest Stewardship Council certified
stock from sustainably managed forests.

Manufactured in China.
Illustrations by Vanessa Balleza.
Design by AJ Hansen.
Typesetting by Maureen Forys, Happenstance Type-O-Rama.

1 3 5 7 9 10 8 6 4 2

The Collective Book Studio®
Oakland, California
www.thecollectivebook.studio

To Maria and Pedro,
who elevate me,
and João, who grounds me.
You're my everything.

Calvin, we miss you.

Contents

Prologue

Calvin never liked to travel, carried around in our hands. His tiny heart would beat against all the bones in his body, making them vibrate—warning us that he wasn't okay.

That's how I know that Calvin belongs here: His heart couldn't handle traveling back to his home country.

🍏

Calvin is a chinchilla. Chinchillas are rodents native to the Andes Mountains in South America. They live in colonies way up high on the mountain slopes. I live in the northern half of Portugal, close to the seashore.

Chinchillas are larger than ground squirrels but have similar tails. They have hind limbs like kangaroos, hands like hamsters, and ears like mice. And their fur is smooth as silk. I have to bury my fingers in Calvin's fur to feel it. That's how soft it is, with more than sixty hairs in a single follicle—the spot where we humans grow only a single hair.

Chinchillas became endangered because of their fur, but they found homes worldwide that kept them safe. I like to think that ours is one of those homes.

When I was a baby, my parents figured I would give them free time by sitting me down to watch Calvin in his cage. I would sit in a baby chair or lie on the floor on my tummy, watching Calvin like he was the best cartoon I could ask for.

Calvin would stay quiet, watching me watch him—his whiskers moving back and forth. Or he'd jump from the ground to the first floor of his two-story cage. He'd use the wooden beam as a launching pad.

Dad installed the beam between the cage bars. With the beam's help, Calvin wouldn't fall as often while moving between floors. Whenever he did fall, I would laugh and laugh. And whenever he fell asleep, I would sleep as well. And most of the time, I'd wake from the noise of Calvin losing his balance after falling asleep on the wooden beam.

My parents shared all the Calvin stories with me. I can't get enough of them to this day.

Calvin was my first friend. From the moment I learned to speak, I would tell him everything about my day. He would give me two things I couldn't get from any person: time to listen to me and silence to let me think.

☙

I was only four and knew exactly what I wanted. And it was all about carrying my chinchilla between my hands, chest, and lap. To Calvin, it must have felt like he was traveling between continents. He went back and forth and back home again.

I brought Calvin closer to me so I could feel him. He smelled like nothing, but I still could sense the wet hay in his fur. His whiskers tickled my face and arms. And his fur felt like a cloud.

I took the fast beating of Calvin's heart as proof of excitement. I didn't know better, only that I loved carrying him. Why wouldn't he love to walk around with me?

"You're making Calvin nervous," Mom once told me as I pulled Calvin out of his cage.

How could that be? I would never do that to my best friend.

I was sure from that moment onward that Mom knew nothing about friendships. She knew nothing about Calvin and me. And she knew nothing about the strength of the bond that connected us.

So, I took Calvin outside to our backyard, which left Mom nervous.

"Amelia, come back inside with Calvin," Mom said, following me. "Immediately."

But I didn't go back inside. I didn't even turn to eye Mom and the look of the wild sea she carries on her forehead whenever she gets nervous or upset. I went on and on, straight to the shade of our sugar apple tree. It always calmed me down, and I was sure it would also calm Calvin. I freed Calvin in my lap and touched him with a leaf from the sugar apple.

Calvin's pink nose and whiskers traveled a thousand miles per hour. Up and down. Up and down. And side to side sometimes, too. And after all the movements ended, Calvin's heart silenced. It must have been because Calvin and the sugar apple are from the same place.

Sugar apples are the fruit of *Annona squamosa*. It's a tree that comes from the high regions of the Andes Mountains (Ecuador, Bolivia, and Peru), just like chinchillas.

I wouldn't say sugar apples are pretty. They're dark green on the outside, and their skin is like fish scales. The skin is thin and delicate, though, and grows invisible fur that makes them smooth to the touch.

Sugar apples hang from the branches like they're going to fall. But they stay there—stubborn—for a long time. They grow big but are hard to spot. The dark green leaves hide them like secrets on a treasure map.

I could live in the Andes, even if I've never been there. After all, the Andes region brought me two things I love and admire: my sugar apple tree and Calvin. They would share their home with me, just like I share my home with them. That's what friends do for each other. Although, I don't take it for granted.

Mom arrived in our backyard a few minutes after I sat down with Calvin. She stopped next to us and couldn't believe her eyes.

Calvin had fallen asleep in my hands on top of a sugar apple leaf. Maybe she thought he was dead. Mom never told me that, but I could hear her heart beating outside her chest and her breathing getting heavier. Both her heart and breathing became smoother when she realized Calvin was okay. And I was okay, too.

Mom probably didn't want me to hold a dead animal in my hands when I was four. But even though I'm ten now, not much has changed.

Chapter 1

Friends are supposed to keep their promises instead of changing plans at the last minute. The talent show should have been fun—my finest moment. But it didn't turn out that way.

And now I'm stuck here, on the cold floor of the girls bathroom at Vera Cruz Middle School, sobbing my eyes out. I should be onstage listening to the applause after singing and dancing in the talent show with Camila—being a part of the effort to improve our school. The money from the show tickets will be used to build a climbing wall at the playground.

Dad once told me that it's okay to feel whatever I feel. It all comes down to what I choose to do about it. But he forgot to tell me exactly *what* that choice might be.

I couldn't react when Camila's decision to act solo fell into my lap like a bomb. All I could do was grow bubbles in my throat and make it impossible for me to swallow, breathe, or talk. *Not much of a talent!*

While I was choking, Camila went into a quick rehearsal of her new performance. She acted as if nothing had happened. Camila's a pro at singing and dancing, so it's easy for her. She's been in classes since she was in preschool.

"If it's hard for you, Amelia, we can each do our own act," Camila said. "You can do whatever you're comfortable with, and we won't get disqualified."

I stood there, my mouth wide and still, incapable of making sounds. The fog on my glasses grew upwards. The bubbles living inside my throat got massive. And the red of my heart traveled to my cheeks and into my eyes.

"We can't give up," Camila insisted. "Leaving would be worse than giving a bad performance. The show must go on." She waved her arms in the air while balancing on her tiptoes. It was as if she was sharing the biggest insight of her life. Without realizing it, Camila showed me a way out.

My face was quickly turning persimmon-red. The girls bathroom wasn't that far away. While everyone was at the school's show, no one would be there.

Before my mind had time to think it further, my body ran. I was superfast.

🍎

"Amelia, are you in there?"

My parents have found me. My brother, Lucas, trails behind them. It's a bittersweet feeling: My heart goes from distressed to a mix of comfort and anger. Like when you fill your mouth with a huge bite of a juicy, sour green apple. I want Mom and Dad to stay close now that they're here. Still, I'm not okay with what happened.

"No," I answer. I want to be alone without feeling lonely.

"Amelia, c'mon," Dad says. "It's okay."

"We were expecting to see you in the talent show with the fifth graders," Mom says. I can't see them from inside the stall, but I'm sure Dad's giving Mom his don't-tell-her-that look. She never likes it and tends to ignore it. "Amelia, you want to tell us what happened?"

I don't want to tell them or talk about anything. I only want to forget.

"I'm sick."

I'm not lying. I may not have been sick before the talent show, but I sure feel ill now.

"You'll be okay." Dad is not a talker. Like me, he prefers silent conversations. He enjoys thinking about what comes to his mind and saying nothing about it.

"Let's go home," Dad says.

The invisible ties holding me to the ground loosen. Still, I can't move.

"I want to be alone. I don't want everyone to see me like this."

Mom huffs. "Most people are leaving," she says. "It's getting late. C'mon." She sounds impatient, and my body stiffens.

I want to go back as if nothing happened. I wish I could see Camila and me hugging after nailing our performance together—high up on the stage, smelling a bouquet of roses.

Instead, I'm down on the floor, smelling bathroom smells. All because I have no talent.

I can tell Mom's patience with me is wearing thin. She's embarrassed because I didn't take part in the talent show. That brought her to a boil faster than usual.

Mom's patience is a cliff over a deep, dark pit. If I take one step forward, I'll fall into the unknown. But I don't know what to do. I feel tight inside like I always feel when I'm running out of time to do whatever I must, like leaving this restroom. I'm sure of it when a minute after saying, "C'mon," Mom drops her second *huff*.

I have to make time to breathe and think and act straight. Mom and I measure time differently. I'm lucky my heart fills my head with the thought of Calvin.

Thinking of my chinchilla allows me to back up a few steps from the cliff of Mom's hurry. I gain the strength to get up, even if I have to use both hands to hold each leg. It's like I'm lifting two logs buried in the restroom floor.

I unlock the door, and Mom and Dad pull it open. I don't face them, and no words come. But the moment our eyes meet, I realize they see me as an embarrassment. All the signs are there. I lose all strength in every bone of my body. The tips of my fingers sting. It's as if a wave has washed over me, turned me into liquid, and dragged me into the sand to disappear. Which I wish I could.

I don't want people to see me like this. I can't leave the restroom before everyone leaves the school. And I'm sure people are still around.

"Let's go now," Dad says.

I freeze like an ice statue.

"Amelia?" Dad wraps his large right-hand fingers around my arm and gives me a light pull.

"I can't," I say.

"Now what?" Mom says.

"Everyone will see me like this."

"Like what?" Mom asks.

"Like this, all red. Everybody will know I've been crying."

"You have been crying, Amelia," Mom says. "And besides, it doesn't look like it."

"It does," I say.

"There's no one left, Amelia," Dad says. "Everyone is gone."

"I want to go home," Lucas says. "Now."

Mom huffs and starts leaving us. Lucas runs after her.

Dad's fingers hold my arm as if he means it. He wants me to move, too, but his voice is steady and calm.

"Amelia, you got this." Dad locks his eyes on mine. "There's no one at school now. But if we happen to meet someone, you can do this. I know you can. Breathe for a second."

I go from liquid to a person again. And I breathe.

The air doesn't enter my lungs at first, but Dad keeps eyeing me.

I try again, and a bit more air enters now, and I'm able to close my eyes.

I breathe deeply. My belly rises and falls, big and small, and I focus on that: *breathing*.

My fingers stop stinging, and I hold Dad's hand. It's warm and big.

Dad opens all five fingers and closes his hand around mine like a cocoon.

"Whenever you're ready," Dad says.

I take one step and another. Dad takes the same steps, the same length as mine.

As we're crossing the gate to leave school, I see Mr. Lima from the corner of my eye.

"Amelia?" Mr. Lima asks. "Did you and your parents enjoy the show?"

Dad glances at me. I say nothing.

"It was pleasant," Dad says. "Congratulations to all."

I know I should have said something, Mr. Lima being my teacher and all. My hand sweats inside Dad's, but he says nothing about my silence.

Outside of the school, Dad frees my hand. I let go of the air I didn't know I was holding inside.

Our house is a ten-minute walk away.

Dad and I pass the school's outer wall, walking down the street before we turn left.

Mom's close to the light-blue-walled music school in the corner. I can't see Lucas, and I'm sure Mom's upset. Lucas must be running ahead as he always does, and she doesn't like that.

"I'm running to meet Mom," I tell Dad, and run as fast as I can to reach her before she turns left.

The sidewalk looms ahead of me like a dark-blue and white puzzle. The dark stones show figures that tell stories about the sea and the lives of people that lived here long before we did.

Stones are loose here and there. I jump over the missing spots and the holes left open to fix water and other issues (as Mom and Dad explain).

"I want you to sign me up for music classes," I exclaim as soon as I catch Mom.

The cold from the ending winter fills my words with clouds.

Mom's huff comes with a gigantic cloud. She's in a hurry the minute I get to her. I know she wants to get home quickly, and she takes longer steps than anyone I know—even Dad.

"Or dancing." I try not to sound too forceful.

Mom's forehead wrinkles like a stormy sea as I avoid her gaze. The muscles in Mom's forehead connect to her toes through internal wires like a puppet. I know that because she walks faster when she frowns. My time keeps getting shorter.

"I can't paint onstage," I say.

"You love art classes," Mom says. "You love to paint. Do you want to explain what happened at the talent show?" Mom asks. Her forehead looks smooth and calm.

"Nothing," I answer. "I wasn't feeling well. I'm better now. You may want to let me watch TikTok today."

"Out of the question, Amelia." Mom's forehead returns to a wild sea.

I stop. My arms cross in front of my chest.

Mom's still walking fast. I stare at her, trying to make her stop with my eyes and mind. I have my own storm growing on my forehead. The storm is sliding down the corner of my eyes and chin. It's about to ravage my whole face.

I could have shined today if I had signed up for classes that let me perform on a stage. If I watched TikTok, I could learn and practice dancing as the entire fifth grade does.

As Mom's walking without glancing back, the floor below my white sneakers pulls me inside. How can she be mad at me for being sad?

The bubbles growing in my throat push out a roar-turning-into-a-grunt noise. I sound more like Lucas than myself, meaning Mom will tell me I'm behaving like a six-year-old.

Mom turns back and stares as if she doesn't recognize me. I saw the same look on Camila's face when she proposed a new act. I don't like it, but at least I can see it.

I never saw any looks like that on Calvin's face before he decided to disappear.

As the idea of losing Calvin comes to my mind, it blends with the thought of missing the show. It's too much to hold inside, and I want to throw up.

"Are you okay?" Mom asks.

I nod yes while looking at my feet. I want to be okay.

I'll ask for an explanation as soon as I see Camila. And as soon as I find Calvin. And time can slow down to how it used to be, and we can be friends again.

Chapter 2

Dad opens the door to the corridor we share with five neighbors. It's a straight hall over a flight of stairs, surrounded by white walls.

The outside walls separate everybody's yards. But nature keeps sharing the lives that spread within each of them. At least, that's what I like to think: We build up walls, but nature doesn't care.

People grow cabbages in their gardens, which rise over the top of the outer walls surrounding the houses. Cats travel over the walls and roofs to sit in the shade of the trees and take the best out of each garden. And banana passion fruit grows over the neighbor's wall for us to pick whenever we feel like it.

For a small country, Portugal has many landscapes and all kinds of weather on the same day. Being close to the ocean has something to do with it. Most days, I wake to a low fog that opens to a sunny morning in the Beira Mar neighborhood. Afternoons can be rainy or not, but they're always windy. And there's the river running by. The seagulls and the flamingos come with salty water. As well as the smell of wet algae and moliço. It's like being at the beach without the sand and the sea.

Still standing on the sidewalk, I untie my arms and run as fast as possible.

I pass Mom, stumble on Dad's super large sneakers, and knock Lucas down. He cries as if I do things on purpose, which I don't.

I don't want to stop and make Lucas feel better. I'm not well myself. But I can't leave him either, the way Mom did with me at school.

I stay there, hearing Lucas cry. My fists close tightly, and my nails burn the flesh in my palm. I open my hands wide, stretching all ten fingers and releasing all my strength through my nails in the opposite direction. I breathe and put my right hand over Lucas's left shoulder after he stands up.

"Are you okay?" I ask Lucas. "I didn't mean to push you."

I calm down. My face relaxes, and my lips smile a small smile. I want Lucas to feel good. He shouldn't be miserable just because I am.

"You did it on purpose," Lucas screams.

"What?" I didn't expect to hear that.

"You did," Lucas insists. "You're smiling."

I can't believe my brother. I shouldn't have stopped to make him feel better. No one ever tries to make me feel better.

"I didn't push you on purpose," I shout to Lucas, Mom, Dad, and all the neighbors who care to hear. "I'm sorry, okay?"

"No, you're not sorry," Lucas says. "You did it on purpose."

That's it. I've had enough for today. I won't stay here to apologize if Lucas is not ready to accept it.

I run all the way to the end of the hall. The door to our garden is the first one on the right. But I don't want to stand there, waiting for Mom or Dad to unlock the entrance to the mudroom. And then to open the door into our garden.

I face the wall as I wait for everyone to enter. I don't want to see my family. And I'm sure they don't want to see me either.

I can hear Dad unlocking the second door. Quick as a flash, I race by, pushing past everyone the minute he opens it.

I run through the backyard and pass the orange trees. I pass the medlar tree, which is still pretty small. And I go through the vegetable garden and the little greenhouse under the lemon tree.

I run all the way down to the sugar apple tree.

I stop under the tree and stare up.

I never talk to the tree, but somehow my feet stop there and keep me standing longer than usual. I feel a magnet pulling me to the ground.

Something is stuck in my throat, and I long to free it. But once I open my mouth, nothing comes out. My mouth stays open, my feet keep me bolted to the cement floor, and my eyes don't turn away from the tree.

I shake my head. I haven't had such a good day so far—true—but this is odd.

Whatever is holding me here passes. Maybe it's me.

I take off my sneakers and leave them under the tree, because I forgot to switch to my Crocs.

We're supposed to put on our Crocs to play in the backyard and take them off as we go inside the house. Mom calls these "hygiene rules." Street shoes, like my sneakers, are supposed to be put in the mudroom. But sometimes, Lucas and I forget.

I should have put the sneakers where they belong, but Mom, Dad, and Lucas are still there, and I need to be alone.

I run up the stairs, socks against the cold cement floor until I get inside.

I'm home.

I slam the door, lean against it, and shout, "Calvin!"

Although my mind thinks loudly about the sugar apple tree, I hear silence.

If I could choose to be anything, I'd be a sugar apple. Sugar apples are smart enough not to grow in the tightness of clusters. They're different in an awkward way. They hold tight to their tree and are stubborn enough to stay there. They give us only a few days to eat them once they fall. They need our full attention. And in the blink of an eye, they're gone.

I'm quiet, like a tree.

Calvin's my sugar apple. I can't set him free from my heart. I wish I were someone's sugar apple.

The silence is about to change. I hear Mom, Dad, and Lucas approaching from outside.

For now, the silence breaks into cracks and snaps. I want to hear all the cracks and snaps, so I stay quiet. Where do the sounds come from? Is it Calvin moving around and hiding?

I move away from the door and shout again, "Calvin!"

My voice disappears into the empty silence like a soap bubble bursting alone in a void.

When I hear footsteps right behind the door, I run across the living room. I take the hall next to the kitchen and the stairs up to the second floor.

If I don't get to watch TikTok today, I'm showering first.

Since Calvin disappeared, I like to be the first one to shower. Dad's happy with my decision to bathe first since I'm fast. He says I'm growing up, like the fruit before it falls from the tree. To be honest, all I want is some time for myself away from everyone worrying about what I have to do and when I have to do it, like showering and doing homework.

"You're wasting my time," Dad used to say. "And yours, too."

I used to hate showering once I got home at the end of the day. I guess grown-ups have nothing better to do than run to the bathtub once they get home. But not Lucas and I. *Oh no!* We kids, we know our priorities. We'd have a blast running fast and hard to the sofa, the playroom, or the TV. Or taking our time to take off our jackets, washing our hands, or going to the bathroom.

Things are different now.

"I'll go first," I always say. It makes my brother rush to get in before me, leaving Dad to explain to Lucas that he can shower next. That's because Dad needs to oversee his bath time while Lucas learns to do it himself. Not me. I've been bathing all by myself since I was five.

"I'm happy with both my big kids," Dad always says, making Lucas feel happy for going second.

While Lucas is taking his bath, I go to Mom and Dad's room. The long mirror there lets me see myself from head to toe.

I stand in front of the mirror in my pajamas.

My hair is not long or short, brown or blond. Everybody compliments my big eyes and eyelashes, but I cover them with my glasses. I'm not tall or short, not fat, but also not thin.

I'm *regular*. I'm like anyone else. I wish I could be more like—I *could* be more like Camila. Except now I'm mad at her. And at Dad, Mom, and even myself. I can't say why Camila stands out, but she does. I want to stand out, too.

Actually, I'm a step down from regular. I don't have a phone. I have to ask Dad to put music on his whenever

I need to work on my dance moves. And I'm not going to ask him now. I'll play the music in my head like I do in school.

One thing I'm sure of: I won't stay a regular someone with no talents. I don't want to be the person depending on others to perform on a stage.

🍎

Dad sits on the bed like I'm not there. I'm not dancing in front of him, so I ignore him, go to my room, and close the door. I need privacy.

I open my closet door. A tall mirror hides inside, glued to the door. I have less space to see myself, but it will work.

I remember the steps Camila and I rehearsed for the talent show. I try them out, but they don't work for a solo performance.

I remember watching other girls working on new steps in school.

One arm up and then the other. I jump and cross my legs as I land. I move my body to the sound of the imaginary song that plays inside my head. Clap to the left and the right. No, it's not working.

I give it another try and another. I'm not doing it right. What am I missing? I can't do this. I need classes, or I must watch YouTube videos and copy them. *Something.*

I decide dancing is not my talent. I'll try a different talent tomorrow.

I'm tired of working on my talents for today. So, I go downstairs and sneak into Dad's home office.

Chapter 3

It's twilight. The sun leaks into the dim room. The yellow of the streetlights is about to replace the winter-orange-tinted sunlight, so I don't need to turn the office lights on. I jump over the sofa on the right and use it to help me onto the windowsill. I love watching the street from here. Today, though, there's only a cat running against the cold wind.

I crouch under Dad's desk. There's a zoo of black boxes and wires spread out all over the top. He calls it a working station. It's indeed for working since Dad works from home. It really is a zoo, though, too. That's because Dad writes software. The software allows everyone to watch video feeds on their computers at home. It's like when we watch animals at the zoo.

I crawl slowly. My back rests against Calvin's white two-story cage on the floor next to Dad's desk. My chest tightens.

I hear Dad upstairs with Lucas.

Mom must be reading in the living room. She's always studying something about oral health. She blames having little time on needing to always read for her dental job. That helps keeps the wild sea on her forehead.

I can't hear her, which is a good sign.

"Calvin," I say out loud. "Today was not, I repeat, *not* a good day. We had the talent show I told you about last week. Remember me saying I was performing with Camila? Well, first things first. A talent show: dumbest idea ever. *And* making everyone take part in it? Not all of us have a talent to show onstage. I'm a painter. I'll be a famous painter one day. I'm not a dancer, a singer, or anything that shines onstage. Not today, not ever. How could I paint onstage and still call it a show? Much less a talent show."

I take a breath.

"Second, you'd never guess what happened," I say. "Lucas threw a tantrum when we arrived at school. Mom asked him what happened in front of *EV-ery-one.* Can you imagine that? She didn't ask him in private. I felt sorry for Lucas, but embarrassed by him, too. It took a while for him to stop crying and be all smiley again. We went to the school's gymnasium, where Mr. Lima and teachers from other grades set up the stage. I ran backstage to find

Camila and the rest of my class. It was a mess. Everyone was rehearsing. And teachers were racing around, still finishing last-minute stuff. It looked . . . urgent—like something unexpected could happen at any moment."

Calvin knows I don't like last-minute surprises or changes. They make the bubbles form in my throat that make me want to leave everything behind.

"Third, Camila broke my heart today," I say. "At the last minute, she wanted to do a different routine, and then she decided to do her routine and leave me on my own. Camila wanted to be her own shiny star. She knew she couldn't win with no-talent me. Still, I never thought she'd do that to me. I could use a new, untalented friend. I tried not to make a big deal, but it hurt. It still does. I don't know what to do about it. I hate school. I hate talent shows. I hate that some people have talents to show off while the rest have to work backstage—or wherever we're meant to be. *I'd* never do that to Camila. I'd also never do that to you, either. Why did you have to disappear? Have I been bothering you with my nagging?"

I sigh. The air leaving my lungs steals the words from my mouth, and I welcome the silence. Again. But my mind rips apart the silence by asking the same thing over and over again: *Where are you, Calvin? Please, don't leave.*

My hand runs down my hair without me thinking about it. I guess my hair misses Calvin's tiny paws. I know I do.

I hear his squeaks like he understands my feelings. There's no "no," and there's no "you should do this" or "do that." The perfect squeaks come out of Calvin's stillness when he's paying full attention to what I'm saying.

Calvin used to jump like crazy whenever I entered Dad's office. Or when he lost his balance and fell. Those were the two times he got loud.

I miss his loudness. And I miss the squeaks, although I hear them from time to time. That's why I know, *I'm sure*, he isn't gone—like gone *gone*.

Mom and Dad say he died. I arrived home from school one day, and he was nowhere to be seen. His cage had hay, the rocks I gave him, the wooden house, and the wooden beam. It had my drawings and his water bottle was still filled. But he wasn't there. Calvin was gone. I searched for him all over the house.

Calvin wouldn't leave without saying goodbye. I'm sure of it. He was here in the morning, but the cage was empty when I came home.

My parents must have gotten distracted. They must have opened the cage to feed him. I'm sure they got a phone call or something, so they forgot to close the door. And Calvin ran away from his cage, but not from our home. He must be close by. I'm sure Calvin went for a walk around the house. But he'll return to his cage and to me.

Mom and Dad say he's dead because they can't find any better explanation for losing him. They don't want to fill me with hope. Yet, I can't do anything but hope.

I want to see his long tail again with the hair gap right where it grows from the end of his body. I miss his whiskers, the dark and gentle stare, the pinkish nose, and the ears, including the gnawed one. I miss the white fur on his tummy. Mostly, I miss his tiny paws resting on top of my thumb. He would put them together, as if he was praying, while I scratched his chin with my index finger. I remember his eyes relaxing until they closed—as I relaxed whenever I told him about my day.

Calvin would balance on top of the wooden beam. His tiny paws would reach through the bars to hold strands of my hair—his nose scrunched up as if each smell was a sip of juice.

I curl a strand of hair on my finger to remember my chinchilla.

I miss the wet smell of hay and sawdust, damp from the water dripping from his water bottle. It's all gone. Mom took everything to the garbage and cleaned the cage well. She used dish soap and a sponge to take the smell out. I want the smell back.

Mom said the hay and everything else was rotting. She could replace it with a new batch. Because she hasn't, Calvin would never follow the smell back home. That's why I'm against an empty cage. Calvin will have to follow the sound of my voice back.

"I talk because I miss you, Calvin," I whisper against the silence of the night. "I talk because I believe in you, Calvin. I believe in us. Mom doesn't believe you're alive, but I do. I always will. Please, come back to me."

Dad calls out that it's time for dinner. I guess I lost track of time. The yellow streetlights are on. My eyes were resting on two big teardrops that never fell. I couldn't see because my light-blue glasses always fog up when my eyes decide to either cry a river or get blocked by an invisible dam.

My stomach's heavy, like I swallowed a rock without chewing it. I'm not hungry.

I don't want to answer Dad. I can't push it, though. After what happened at school, I'm sure they won't be happy if I don't show up for dinner.

"I'm coming," I say. But I don't move. Why do my legs grow roots wherever I sit?

It'll be a while until I decide to take each massive log leg off the floor. I'll say I'll be there two or three times more. Dad will feel tired, and Mom's patience will be wearing thin. I know what will happen, but I still can't move.

I close my eyes, and it's like I'm sitting on the floor of the girls bathroom all over again. The bubbles grow inside of my throat, and I get dizzy.

I don't want to have dinner. I want my life back, unchanged, with Calvin at home and Camila at school, performing next to me as we had planned.

"I'm coming," I whisper. I can't find the strength to speak any louder.

I reach under my glasses to wipe the unfallen tears from my eyes. My cheeks burn, and I can tell my face is red. I'll tell Mom and Dad it's from the heat we turn on during winter. I don't want them to know I've been crying, so they don't keep asking me what's wrong.

I move each leg like a crane lifting a beam. I'm up and ready and take slow steps to the living room, prepared to swallow dinner like I'm good. I want to be good.

Chapter 4

Both sugar apples and chinchillas are sensitive to temperature.

I don't like feeling hot myself. I can't ride in the car with my coat on. I know it's a pain to take it off every time I get in, when I only have to put it back on again a few minutes later. But that's me, and sugar apples, and chinchillas. The air needs to flow through our bodies freely.

Once, I slept with a princess outfit over my jammies. It got too hot under the covers, and I woke up in the middle of the night with a fever.

I hate being sick and having a fever. Sometimes, though, it comes in handy.

"It can't be Tuesday already," I tell Mom when she comes to kiss me in the morning.

Mom never misses a good morning kiss, no matter what happened the day before. She gives me a new opportunity to start over each day, which I love. But I can't take the heaviness out of my heart this time.

I'm not sad, but am I still mad? I'm not sure.

"Tuesday it is," Mom says. "Did you sleep well?"

I say nothing and lie in my bed, letting my eyes blur as they watch the foggy sky outside the window.

"Tuesday's a school day. Time to get ready," Mom insists as she drops a kiss on the cheek that's not touching the pillow. Mom leans over me and offers her own cheek. I kiss her back.

"Good morning," I say.

Tuesdays used to be better than Mondays. It's one step closer to the weekend, but far enough away to share plenty of time with Camila at school.

Today's Tuesday is not better than yesterday's Monday. It's actually worse because it's time to face what happened. And I can't do it.

I need time that gets longer, that stretches out. I need it to be long and wide until my heart stops pounding in my chest, searching for a way out. It fails to exit, so it goes up my throat. I swallow it down, but it keeps pushing up. And I hear it loudly hitting in my head: *lub-dub, lub-dub, lub-dub*.

I'm sure I'm sick, and it's a good day to be sick.

"You'll feel better once you get fresh air before your class starts," Mom says when I tell her I'm not feeling well.

Mom loves the fresh morning air. "It clears bad energies," she likes to say.

Mom steps outside to get oranges for breakfast without putting a jacket on. Just like every morning. That's how she starts her days—always too warm. It's odd because she's cold for the rest of the day. She keeps adding extra layers as the hours run by.

"The morning air cures everything," Mom insists.

"There's this thing that was making me sick yesterday," I say in the best way I can to convince her without lying. "The thing is still growing inside of me." I'm not a liar. I can't tell what it is, but something grows inside me each second.

I learned one thing from waking up this morning: "Sleeping on it" doesn't make *it* better. People who say that don't have to face the same people the next day. I try hard not to lie, so they shouldn't lie to me when they say that either.

"It's better if I skip school today," I insist. "It's better for you to decide to keep me home right away. I promise not to bother Dad. I'll stay quiet. If you take me to school and they call Dad to pick up his sick daughter after a while, it'll only interrupt his work."

"I'll take my chances," Mom says while working to get Lucas out of bed.

Lucas is always dead in the mornings. Mom's entire face scrunches every time she wakes him up. He doesn't care, though. I'm pretty sure I've never seen his forehead wrinkle from anything else but sunlight in his eyes. At least I have my glasses for protection from that.

I stay in my dark-blue jammies, watching them and trying to figure out how to convince her I'm right. I need more time. Also, I need my glasses. Since I have neither, I sigh and take my hurting heart and body to the bathroom to prepare for my worst day.

As I go through what happened yesterday, I'm throwing water on my face. I recall the terrible moments. The thoughts fill my mind like I'm remembering a bad dream. It is no good to remember.

I close my eyes and throw more water on my face. And more. I don't mind the cold. I make a puddle around me.

I open my eyes, straighten my head, and watch myself in the mirror. The water drips onto my pajamas until I feel the wetness on my skin.

Why do I have to go to school?

I dry my face and neck with a towel. I choose a dry towel corner to soak up as much water as I can from my pajamas.

I hang the towel before I remember the wet floor. Now my sock is damp. Could this day get any worse? I'm tired already.

I use toilet paper to dry the floor and leave the bathroom before messing up something else.

I take my clothes to Mom and Dad's room. I like to see myself in their mirror before heading downstairs for breakfast. Standing here reminds me of last night when I tried to be a better dancer. I can't tell why it didn't work because I always dance with Camila at school.

I stand tall in front of my reflection. Ready? One hand up, then the other. Hand on hip, move my body. No, this isn't working for me. Not at all! I lost my dancing ability. It isn't for me anymore. I'll never be talented.

Downstairs I can hear Mom bustling here and there. She's doing the dishes, and I'm sure she'll make fresh juice after.

It's time for breakfast, and I can help her. *Yes!* I can help her with the juice and toast or cook scrambled eggs—we all like those. And it's a talent—an awesome one! I watch a lot of cooking shows on TV. It's a long shot, but I can make it work for a talent show.

I fly down the stairs and into the kitchen in less than a second.

"What?" Mom shouts. "Is something wrong?" I guess I scared her.

"No," I say. "All good. I want to help you with breakfast."

"That's nice," Mom says. "Make sure you wake up earlier tomorrow, and we'll prepare it together."

"What?" I ask. "Why?"

"Don't you want to learn?" Mom says.

"Sure," I say. "I can learn now."

"We don't have time now, Amelia," Mom says. "Plus, I'm done here. Please, take your seat at the table next to your brother."

I can't wait. Learning to cook is the only thing that will make me feel better today.

I stand behind Mom, pretending I didn't hear her. I wait a few minutes before moving next to her.

Mom doesn't notice me. She's working on the toast while closing the fridge and opening the microwave at the same time. She drops two pieces of toast on the plate. I take the knife that rests on top of the butter, pass it through to grab some, and spread it on one toast.

Mom touches me with her elbow and turns around.

"What are you doing?" Mom asks.

"I'm making the toast," I answer. "I'm helping you."

"No, Amelia," Mom says. "That's your brother's toast. He wants honey on it. Yours is already at the table. Please sit there and eat your food before it gets cold."

"Mamã, I want to help," I say. "I need to learn."

"Tomorrow," Mom says. Her look tells me she's not kidding.

I can't do anything right. Tomorrow Mom won't wake me up early to help with breakfast. And I don't know if I'll be able to get up earlier on my own. It's hard as it is. Besides, what else will make me feel better today?

I sit at the table. I have no choice. Mom doesn't stop staring.

I can hardly eat breakfast, but I make space for Mom's fresh orange juice. I don't believe the fresh morning air will cure my inside blues. But I don't want to hurt her feelings either. I sip each drop of juice. I end up with the ordinary "Ah." I tend to give her a big "Ahhhhhh." This tim,e though, I give her a shorter one for not letting me stay at home when I don't feel good. And for not letting me help with breakfast. Or anything I want.

I can't believe I'm heading back to school—still untalented.

Chapter 5

When I finish breakfast, I clean the table and drag myself upstairs to wash my teeth.

"Faster," Mom calls from the kitchen. "Do you both want to be late for school?"

I don't know about Lucas, but I don't mind being late today.

Lucas gets ready and heads to the backyard. Dad's waiting for him in the mudroom.

I leave the house, too, fighting the invisible rust delaying each step forward.

Walking under the sugar apple tree to the mudroom, something is messing with my hair.

I stop and take my hand over my head to pick up the leaf that got stuck there.

I watch the leaf in my hands, fresh and green. Sugar apple trees don't lose their leaves before spring. But the weather keeps changing, so maybe they will fall earlier this year. I see no other sugar apple leaves spread on the ground. Not a single one.

I caress the softness of the leaf before putting it in my pocket. Touching it makes me feel better and may help me get through the day.

One step forward and a gust of wind surprises me and whirls more leaves around me. Over my head, a cluster dances its way down to the ground, falling at my feet.

Lucas makes a lot of noise in the mudroom. I can hear Dad getting impatient.

I'm not in a hurry. Not today.

I count the leaves as I pick them up one by one. There are twenty in my hand, and I throw them up like fireworks before running to the mudroom to meet Dad and Lucas.

The morning air rushing over my face, clothes, and backpack doesn't make me feel better like Mom said it would. When I arrive at the school's gate, I'm feeling worse. If I tilt my head up, I can loud-gurgle all the bubbles inside my throat. I don't want people to stare, though. Especially after not having any talent to present at yesterday's long-awaited show.

My hand travels to my pocket to feel the leaf before going through the gate.

Twenty-one leaves, I count to myself. Not twenty. Twenty at home. Twenty-one when I add this one. Twenty-one like Calvin.

A chill rushes up my spine, which scares and excites me at the same time. The tree, my tree, remembers Calvin's age.

I gain the strength to enter.

Once inside, the bell rings, and I speed to class. Everyone's there except for Mr. Lima. The noisy-kid sounds bounce out into the hallway.

Everyone's out of their seats, huddled together in a tight mass.

I can't spot Camila in the group.

The noise is the same as every morning, except this time I'm not part of it. And today it's all about talents. I catch snippets of the words lost in the air. They might as well throw them at my face. *Show. Great. Success. Congrats. Happy. Performance.*

I don't hear *loser* or *coward*, but I might as well have. The words would be valid. People don't have to hide their thoughts. I hear them bursting inside my head. *C'mon. Go ahead and get in there.* I'm tough as nails.

I realize I don't see Camila because she's holding everyone's attention. She's at the center of the buzz, in the middle of the crowd. Camila's smiling and answering questions about her performance.

Okay, I'm not tough as nails. I'm soft as snails. And I want to turn my back away from this never-ending show and go home.

No one asks me what happened yesterday. Nobody talks to me, Camila included. Everyone's absorbed in Camila. It's like they are drowning in her illusion of fame. They don't care about what didn't happen, like me missing the show.

I choose to think it's a good thing. It's like I died and was reborn as a sugar apple.

Sugar apples are big. Yet, you can hardly see them hanging from their tree. They're brilliant in their disguise, showing only the same green as the leaves that hide them.

Mr. Lima enters. He shushes the noise until it's close to silence. Everyone slowly takes their seats, me included.

I can tell Mr. Lima has an announcement to make. Whenever he does, the corners of his lips round up in a disguised smile.

"Set your books aside," Mr. Lima says. "Today, you're going to write about what unique talent you have, and how you presented it at the school's talent show."

Oh no! Please tell me I'm still a sugar apple and he can't find me. Please don't ask about my talent. What did I miss between yesterday and today? The world is nothing but skills and shows. I need a new friend and a new teacher now, too.

I can't help but frown. Mr. Lima asks me what's the problem. So much for my sugar apple self.

"I have no talents," I explain to Mr. Lima. "It's okay, though. Once I have one, I'll let you know and finish the assignment." I try to explain it to him with patience, as I like people to do with me, whether they have time or not

"Obrigado, Amelia—thank you—but it's mandatory." Mr. Lima likes to be precise. "Please write about a talent you'd like to have for today's class. After all, dreaming is in itself the most powerful talent!" He finishes with a rounded smile as if he struck gold.

I must be staring at him like he's performing his own private talent show, because he clears his throat. He turns away with a single eyebrow raised.

I take my pencil, eraser, and exercise book. I struggle to organize my mind but soon I'm ready to start.

"I have no talents," I write down in my notebook. *"At least, no talents I can show on the stage of a talent show. And I'm*

thinking hard about having no single talent. I've explained it to Mr. Lima, my fantastic teacher, although I didn't have to. Everyone watched me run away from the school's talent show. Or at least people noticed I was gone, since Camila performed alone. And we always rehearsed together. The entire school knows how hard we practiced during breaks. I guess Camila is the top talent of the team."

I hope Mr. Lima appreciates me telling him how great he is.

I like it so far. I review the spelling and keep writing.

"If I could choose a talent, I'd like to be able to make others forget. Especially grown-ups. They love to talk things through. They push to understand what you feel. I know what I feel. I don't have to say it; they don't have to hear it from me. It's funny how nobody asks me to say it out loud when I'm fine. It's different when I'm sad. Grown-ups always need to know if I'm sad. They want to understand what happened. And the absolute worst thing is they want me to think about what I can do to make it different the next time."

I take a breath.

"If people think it through, they'll know I'm right. First, talking about sad things only reminds us of what made us sad. Remembering sad things makes everyone sadder. Dad always says that while

watching the news. Second, understanding what happened doesn't change it. You can't go back in time. Third, I don't know how to fix it for next time. If I did, I probably wouldn't have made the mistake the first time."

Mr. Lima walks around and asks students if they need help. I don't look up, and he doesn't stop near me. My time stretches out when people aren't pressuring me.

I keep writing. My hand feels like it has gained a will of its own.

"This is why I didn't answer my dear teacher, Mr. Lima, when he asked me about the talent show when I left to go home yesterday."

I don't answer Mom and Dad when they ask me what I do in the home office every night, either. Why do they have to know? People ask me about sad things I can only feel, not explain. The words become hard in my heart and dry in my mouth.

I need an ending. Mr. Lima says a good text needs a beginning, a middle, and an end. The beginning introduces the theme or problem. I made mine clear: Talking things out makes me sad, and I want to make people forget and ask me nothing. My middle is good because I explain why people shouldn't question certain things.

I take my sparkly purple pencil in my right hand again and start on my conclusion.

"This is why I want to have the talent to make others forget. If I could make others forget already, no one would remember the talent show. I could have no talents and act as if nothing happened."

I'm happy with my assignment. I hope Mr. Lima will be, too. And Mom and Dad, as well—when I show them. I hope they stop bugging me about being in Dad's home office, where I talk my feelings out to a lonely cage.

Chapter 6

I put my pencil down and look around. Heads are down; the other kids are still working on their assignments. I'm never first, but I'm the only person here with so little to write. I'm the one who ran away from the talent show, after all.

This assignment must be exciting for everyone who showed off onstage. I wish I were one of those people. I wish I was thrilled to write about any of my talents and the experience of presenting them to others. I'm not one of them.

I sit up. The sky is turning blue outside the window to my left. That's all I can see.

After a minute, Mr. Lima calls me to his desk. What does he want from me?

I move my chair softly because I don't want to distract the rest of the class. And I walk to Mr. Lima's desk.

"You're finished?" Mr. Lima asks me.

"I think so," I say.

"Bring it over," Mr. Lima says.

I walk away to pick up the exercise book and hold it in my hand long after reaching Mr. Lima.

"Can I read it?" Mr. Lima asks.

My eyes travel from Mr. Lima to the assignment to Mr. Lima and the assignment again.

Mr. Lima stretches out his arm with an open hand. He has a friendly smile on his face.

"Can you read it later?" I ask. "When you're alone."

Mr. Lima drops his hand to the table, keeping it open but palm down. I can hear a sigh escaping through his smile until it vanishes.

"Sure," Mr. Lima says. "You can leave the assignment here." He points at an empty spot at the corner of the table.

The organized desk unfolds like it's a new sight to me. There's a spot for everything, each object not touching the other. Everything sits out in an unknown order, as if held in place by an invisible force.

What would happen if Mr. Lima or I sneezed? I imagine all the papers coming to life and flying away like my sugar apple leaves this morning.

"Did you have a hard time working on your assignment?" Mr. Lima is not giving up.

"I thought it would be harder," I say. "Starting was the hard part."

"Good," Mr. Lima says. "What happened yesterday?"

I freeze. I should have asked Mr. Lima to read the assignment right here and now. I wouldn't have to explain myself that way. It's too late now.

I feel the bubbles climbing up my throat.

"Nothing," I say. "I wasn't feeling well."

"Are you better now?" Mr. Lima asks.

"Yes." I force myself to smile. I need Mr. Lima to believe that I'm okay and leave me be.

"Do you want to talk about what made you ill yesterday?" Mr. Lima asks.

"My stomach was hurting," I say. "Nothing much. I'm sorry for not telling you before."

"When?" Mr. Lima asks.

"When you asked," I say.

Mr. Lima's face shows me he doesn't remember it.

"Before leaving school," I clarify. "Yesterday."

Mr. Lima avoids me. His eyes go through everything spread on his table and to the window before landing on me again.

"You know, Amelia," Mr. Lima adds, "not everyone has to show off. In a show, as in life, the hidden spots are as important as the ones the audience sees."

What does Mr. Lima mean by hidden spots? Was it a good thing I hid in the restroom after all?

"Okay," I say.

"And there's nothing to be sorry about."

My smile widens.

"Thank you," I say.

Mr. Lima watches me with a slight smile. I keep my eyes busy by looking at my hands, feet, and anything else that will keep me from facing him. He sighs again, sends me to my seat, and asks me what I want to do while I wait for the others to finish.

I know he'd love me to choose to read, but the truth slips out faster than I can control it.

"Drawing," I say.

Mr. Lima nods and lets me go.

My chair makes a lot more noise than it did when I got up. Mr. Lima clears his throat, as he sometimes does when he's not happy with something. It's like he has something stuck there and can't get rid of it. I keep my eyes on the table and try to be more careful.

I take my drawing notebook from my bag and open it on the desk. I hold my purple pencil in my right hand.

I think hard about what I'm going to draw, but nothing comes to mind. It's usually easy for me to start drawing. Like it's part of who I am—an extension of my arm and hand. Right now, I'm stuck.

I drop the pencil and place my hand inside my pocket. My fingers travel over the smooth leaf that's protected in there.

I take hold of the pencil again and draw the leaf as I imagine it.

I work with the pencil to draw the invisible fur I feel whenever I touch the leaf. It's not going well.

I can't draw invisible fur. I give up and instead keep drawing until it's not a leaf anymore. It's the tail of a chinchilla.

My chest tightens, and I let out a sigh. It comes out louder than I'd like to, and I can't tell if anyone heard. I keep my eyes on the table.

I stop the pencil from drawing, letting it stick to the paper until I forget my loud breathing.

"There's nothing in there for a young girl," I remember Mom and Dad nagging me after spending time in Dad's home office. "Why do you spend that much time there on your own? You could be reading a book in the comfort of your bedroom."

On my own, they say! Alone! I'm not alone when I'm close to Calvin. I don't care if he's not in his cage. That's because I'm sure Calvin isn't dead. He's taking a walk around the house or the garden and will return anytime. Soon.

I draw the chinchilla's body next to the tail. I try to make it just right, but it doesn't look how I remember Calvin.

I erase the drawing and try it again. You could tell it was a chinchilla, but it looked nothing like my Calvin.

My eyes fill with tears, but I clean them immediately. I don't want anyone to see me crying.

This can only mean that I'm forgetting Calvin. Whenever I think of him, the image in my head is perfectly clear—as if I were with him daily. Why can't I draw him?

The bell rings. It's lunchtime.

Everyone puts their assignment down, and the chairs creak against the floor as the kids hurry to leave the classroom.

Mr. Lima doesn't complain this time. He goes from desk to desk, picking up each assignment except mine, which is already waiting at his desk.

I haven't left when he approaches my seat.

"Mr. Lima," I say. "Can I ask you something?"

"Sure," Mr. Lima says.

"When we love something, is it possible to forget it?"

"Well . . ." Mr. Lima hesitates. "I wouldn't say forget. It's always in our mind and heart, but we may not remember every detail."

I stare at my desk.

"Is everything okay, Amelia?"

I look up and smile.

"Yes," I answer. "I'm fine." I focus on being persuasive.

I leave the classroom to head outside.

The school's playground spreads around the building. There's a central area everyone calls "the cube." It's cube-shaped, surrounded by glass walls, except for the ceiling, which is open-air.

I stand there, staring outside, where everyone's busy with something.

My mind is as busy and puzzled as the life that spreads within the cube.

I'm not giving Calvin enough of my time. I don't want to forget him.

Chinchillas have almost no smell. Just like sugar apples. They both let other scents come alive.

That's why Calvin's cage is special: Despite the cleaning and scrubbing, it keeps the smells that remind me of Calvin and will guide him back home. When it's gone, there's nothing left to remember.

Why did Mom have to clean the cage? She left only my drawings, which I made for Calvin when I was about Lucas's age. And the food bowl and the water bottle. Why don't Mom and Dad talk about Calvin anymore? Why does it feel like they avoid the subject?

Oh no! It hits me. I'm running out of time, and I can't keep waiting anymore. I lose my breath. Although it's evident in my eyes, I go deaf and mute: Mom got rid of everything inside Calvin's cage because she'll get rid of the cage. I have to stop her.

Chapter 7

There has to be a way to keep Calvin's cage. And although I can't think of any ways to stop it, I won't fail him.

I leave the building through the cube and turn left to the basketball court.

Most fifth graders enjoy the court. It's big and perfect for shooting baskets and running back and forth. It's crowded most days, but Camila and I found the ideal spot for rehearsals. It's near the air conditioning ducts. We call it "our spot." It can be noisy, but we're used to dancing to imaginary music, anyway. We're so good when we practice, it's like we could be onstage right then—despite the balls hitting the ground and the *vroom vroom* of the air conditioners. They drown out the songs from the sparrows, the seagulls, and the swallows in the air. But not our singing!

I can't find Camila at our spot. I go back to the lunchroom to see if she's waiting in line already. Camila's not there either.

Where is she?

There's a loud noise coming from the cube. I turn around.

A large group of kids walks toward me. Most of them are from my class. They're chatting, laughing, singing, and twirling. Of course, Camila's with them! She's there, in the center of the world. And I'm here, alone. I'm a lost planet searching for a star to circle, so I can find meaning in my day.

"It was a hit," I hear them talking over each other, each more excited than the other. "I heard Mr. Lima saying we raised enough money to build the climbing wall at the playground. Enough and *more!* And it's only the beginning. We should go on tour and skip school every day. Wow! I can picture us already."

Mom would huff at all this chatter.

A climbing wall. What for? Who wants to climb? We have trees already, and who climbs those? No one. Why? The rules say so. Why do we want to have a wall to climb and do what teachers already forbid? I understand this school less and less. Grown-ups don't stand by their rules. And do they talk about it? No. Do they want to talk about it? I'm afraid not. It'd make them sad to admit they're not sticking to their word.

The group comes closer and closer. I take a few steps ahead to get closer to Camila.

"Camila," I say. She doesn't hear me. I stand firm, louder. "Camila!"

Camila laughs and tosses her curled brown hair at me like I'm a boring fan. She doesn't see me. She has an audience already.

This girl might as well be in an actual spotlight because she's already dressed for it. She struts in her sparkling silver boots, black tulle skirt, and polka-dotted top.

This is someone who doesn't only *look* like she's onstage. She *acts* like she's there already, all smug with her chest puffed out.

Camila smiles just enough to show all her teeth and not show her dimples. Her cheeks are pink enough to look like she has makeup on, but her face is still plain enough to make me think she's my simple Camila.

Yet, she's not my Camila anymore. And this is one stage we'll never share. I'm not part of it, and she's making that clear. Camila looks at me, barely glancing up, even though I stand right in front of her.

"Camila!" I shout. The sleeves of my blue-and-white hoodie cover my hands. I put them on the hips of my regular blue jeans. I shake my normal, straight light-brown hair to appear confident. The lenses of my glasses fog up from the heat rising from my cheeks. I'm not a star, but she can't ignore me.

"What?" Camila says as if I'm calling her for the first time. "Where were you?"

I grab her hand to pull her away from the flock. She stiffens, and I can't pull her too far.

"What?" I ask. "Where were *you*? I searched everywhere for you. You weren't at our spot. I came here thinking you already had lunch."

"No," Camila says. "Where were you yesterday? You missed the talent show. You were supposed to go after me. Didn't you prepare something to show? Everyone was there but you."

"I wasn't feeling well," I say. "Can we talk about something else?"

"Okay, I guess," she says. "Are you better today?"

"I am."

"Ready to try a different song together?" Camila's enthusiasm used to infect me right away, but not this time. I'm not into it. I need to address the obvious: I have no talents.

"Tomorrow," I say. "Let's do something else."

"Like what?" Camila asks.

"Dunno. Any ideas?"

We stand there, eyes on the floor, like two strangers who just met. We've known each other our entire lives. What's wrong? How can a stupid talent show stand between Camila and me? We're much more than that. We can do many different things besides performing. If only I could remember one. What did we do before spending every lunch break dancing and singing, and dancing and singing? *Think, Amelia!*

But I can't. The silence melts my brain as it stretches for over a minute.

I usually like silence and want it to stretch out. This is the one time I wish it were shorter. I want someone to break the silence and turn this moment into something else. Right now, it's weird and uncomfortable.

"Why don't you ask the group if someone wants to practice with you today?" I say, lifting my chin toward the flock, still chatting and waiting a few steps behind us.

"Are you sure?"

"Sure, sure," I say. "I'll go and do something else today for a change."

Camila stands before me, staring at me, either like she pities me or doesn't know me. I can tell she's as anxious to leave as I am. There has to be more than talking about talents and shows. And more than practicing dancing and singing. I'm done with both.

I watch her go, her curled hair shining like a perfect star's.

I sit on my usual chair in the lunchroom. It's odd to be here by myself. Camila's always next to me.

"Hello there, my good eater," Miss Paula, the lunch lady, greets me like she always does.

Miss Paula watches for the bad eaters. She's kind enough to make sure everyone eats plenty and stays healthy. And she's short enough to blend in among us.

Miss Paula frightens some, though—especially the bad eaters. They don't know her like I do. Most kids don't want Miss Paula to see they don't eat because they don't like the food. Or they don't want to get caught talking instead of eating.

I'm not afraid of Miss Paula. Oh no! That's because, first off, I'm a good eater. She's right about that. I like everything, from soup to salad, and all kinds of fruit. Second, I grew three inches last year. I'm about as tall as Miss Paula, now. And despite her red hair and spooky, dark glasses, I like her. Today, she makes me feel less alone.

"Where's the other half?" Miss Paula asks me. "Your friend left you to eat alone today?"

"I was too hungry to wait." I smile without showing my teeth. My cheeks are packed like a squirrel. It's polite to keep my mouth shut when I'm eating. Dad bugs me about that all the time. "Today's spaghetti is the best," I say, hoping to get a smile back.

"Are you okay, kiddo?" Miss Paula asks like she's guessing. Worse, like she's reading my mind. It freaks me out. Why wouldn't I be okay? I haven't told her anything.

I give Miss Paula my best polite smile, hoping she stops staring into my eyes—straight into my soul.

My heart hurts, and bubbles grow inside my throat, leaving no space to eat the rest of the pasta.

"Uh-huh," I mumble, staring at my plate.

"Okay," Miss Paula says. "Eat up. Come and see me in the kitchen if you feel like chatting."

"Sure," I say, although I know I'm not stepping into the kitchen. Not today, not ever. I'm not going to talk about sad things. Not with Miss Paula. Not with any other person.

Tears start to swell in my eyes like a faucet about to turn on. I scan my plate and work hard to swallow the tears with my eyelashes. None fall. I take a breath.

I'll talk to Calvin when I get home. My Calvin.

I think about Calvin each second of each minute. He has to be home when I arrive after school. *Please be home!*

I finish my green-yellowish apple, slurping up the juice that insists on dripping. This apple makes me happier than talking to Miss Paula, Mr. Lima, and Camila. It's sweet and juicy.

I get up only after making sure Miss Paula is distracted by the kitchen and the other kids. I'm free to stop worrying and hurry outside.

I'm not sure where to go. I don't remember being this lonely at lunch break, and it's about time I find a new friend. Life around me is divided into groups: small flocks with fixed rules. I'm not sure if I fit or if they'll let me fit. Two things I'm sure of. First, I'm not going to the basketball court or anywhere close to "our spot." Second, I need a plan that convinces Mom to keep Calvin's cage. And that's urgent.

Chapter 8

Nature protects us all. But it also makes us tough enough to stay alive.

Sugar apples divide themselves into many seeds. I can't eat one without putting it all in my mouth—seeds and all. I suck the sweet white pulp in and spit the black seeds out. It's important not to swallow many of the seeds. Still, humans found their way around that—learning to spit them out.

Chinchillas have their teeth. But if they don't wear them down on hard surfaces, like wood, their teeth can grow into their brains and hurt them.

There's a way around everything.

The same is true for me: I must learn to exist alone without being lonely or finding a friend. That's why I'm trying to get used to being alone, and I like it.

Okay, I don't like it that much. Someone should have warned me about this.

Yesterday came like a nasty surprise. I wasn't expecting to be by myself all day. Camila didn't tell me that she was all about *her* talent *all* the time. And I never realized I have no skills.

I miss having a friend.

The feeling travels with me until I get to school, where everything's the same and different all at once.

The air is full of anxiety around people and things. It's everywhere. It's like glitter falling through the air, twirling and whirling around us.

Whatever it is, it's not about the talent show. No one is talking about it.

Mr. Lima is trying to be his usual, peaceful, full-of-things-to-teach way. But his eyes wander away from us all the time. He can't stop glancing at the door. He almost looks like he's nervous. And I don't know why he's acting like that.

There's a louder-than-usual buzz in the classroom. That's because Mr. Lima is not giving us his full attention.

My mind fights its own buzz of missed shows, lost friends, and a can't-lose cage. And now I'm distracted myself. And nervous. And I can't get back to feeling normal again.

Please look at us, Mr. Lima. And bring the air of anxiety and the noise down. And everything back to where and how it's supposed to be.

Despite the noise, I hear footsteps coming closer to the classroom.

I hope it's not the principal. Will Mrs. Santos come to talk to the students who were missing from the talent show? But it was only me! Were there others?

The footsteps get closer, and the buzz goes crazy. I have a strange feeling.

Mr. Lima is staring past our heads, straight to the door. I can hear his deep breathing from the front row. My breathing is shallower but faster.

Footsteps. Breathing. The air is spinning. Footsteps. Closer. Breathing. Faster. The air whirls around me, and I'm getting dizzier and dizzier.

While Mr. Lima looks more and more unsteady, as if expecting something to happen, three people show up at our door.

"I'm sorry to interrupt," the principal says.

She's not interrupting. Mr. Lima's attention is long gone. Our minds float wildly around the unseen glitter falling through the thick air. Except we sit still like we're paying attention. And Mr. Lima stands straight at the front of the classroom like he's teaching the lesson. My heart falls to my feet. Is Mrs. Santos here for me?

Mrs. Santos tosses her red hair and smiles. It's the shortest smile ever. It stretches and shortens in the blink of an eye. I'm sure she'd win if there were a contest for the fastest smile.

Mrs. Santos can't stay still, regardless if she's the principal. It's like she's always tense, which means she should be solid and static. But she isn't, even though she's everyone's boss, including the teachers.

Being the queen of this school, Mrs. Santos must always think of rules for everyone to follow. Thinking about all of those orders and making sure people follow them must turn her body into a jellylike state that's always on the move.

"This is Iris," Mrs. Santos says. "She's new to our school. And she's thrilled to meet us all." I bet the last part is not true. She knows nothing about us, and Iris's face proves I'm right about that.

The entire class stares back, and I'm able to breathe again. The principal is not here for me. And Mr. Lima seems less anxious. It feels like peace has returned.

The door acts like the frame of a painting. It shows three people standing with three awkward trying-to-be-nice-but-not-sure-how-to-feel smiles.

Mrs. Santos is tall, colored in red, from her hair to her lips and cheeks. Her teeth sometimes show red spots here and there, so I actually prefer her when she's serious.

A lady is standing between Mrs. Santos and Iris. She's about the same height as the principal, but somehow looks taller.

The lady's hair is dark and straight, like a dark brown sheet of paper. Her eyes are as deep and dark as her hair. She reminds me of a bottle turned upside down, with wide hips that narrow into tiny feet below. It's almost cartoonish. A smile forms on my lips, and I can't take my eyes off her.

And there's Iris. She looks so much like the lady that she has to be her daughter. Still, I don't dare guess. "It's bad manners to ask about personal matters," Mom would say.

I scan Iris for any sign of talent: All I can see is a regular girl like me in her light jeans and cool sweater. She doesn't sparkle in any particular way, and her hands fall to her sides and never rest on her hips. Not once.

"Class, please welcome Iris," Mr. Lima says.

"Olá, Iris," we all say.

"Iris is arriving from Madeira," Mr. Lima says. "She flew in yesterday, ready to learn with us. Also, she can teach us about the islands."

Iris turns as red as Mrs. Santos's hair. In a weird way, the red on her face balances this awkward painting.

"Iris, please take the empty seat." Mr. Lima shows Iris her new seat, far in the back row.

Iris moves slowly as her eyes fall to the floor and she lets go of her mom's hand. It's hard to watch. It reminds me of Mom and how she kisses me every morning, Dad and how peaceful he can be, and Lucas and how big his smile gets. And, of course, Calvin and how his whiskers tremble.

I understand this girl. Iris is getting too much attention. It can be embarrassing, especially when Mr. Lima says she can teach us stuff. I know I'd be. Also, I'm sure she's sad about leaving her home behind. But Iris seems like she's a nice sad, not angry sad.

Iris sits in her chair. I can't tell what she brought in her bag, but I'm guessing it's empty. She doesn't open it to take anything out.

With nothing to do with her hands, she takes a small strand of hair behind her left ear. She curls it in her left index finger with the help of her thumb. And when I'm thinking I can't believe my eyes and stop staring, Iris brings her right hand to the table. She takes it from the pocket of her jeans and drops a small white stone on the desk.

The stone sits there. It's small and alone, like a pearl. Until Iris finally reaches into her backpack to take out a sea-shell and a leaf. She lines all three of them up on the table and looks straight at Mr. Lima.

Iris makes no eye contact with any of the kids in the class. And she takes nothing else from the bag: not a book, a notebook, or even a simple pencil.

I like Iris already, especially with the bonus of having someone who doesn't know about the talent show.

I take a deep breath. I'm feeling good. No dizziness. Good and ready.

I haven't found any talent still, and I could use a friend—a kind friend with things in common, like the leaf and the curled hair on the finger. My heart lightens, and my face does too. I can't help the smile that forms on my lips as I plan the possibilities ahead. I forget all about the nervousness eating my insides.

The sky outside the window is blue. I can't see any tree-tops, but I bet there's no wind. And even if there is, I bet it's soft and smells like spring.

It's all good.

I'm going to teach Iris to be my friend, and this Wednesday may turn into a beautiful day after all.

Chapter 9

I have a feeling I can get along with Iris. So, I design a plan in my mind.

It's all I have now: this new and weird feeling that's giving me confidence. And despite the risk of Iris not liking me, I'll take my chances. I have nothing to lose.

Although I have no talents to show off onstage, I keep telling myself I'm doing well. Because I need to think so, despite being alone.

When Mrs. Santos and the must-be-Iris's-mom-lady leave, everyone stares at Iris. At least, that's what I think. I'm already facing Mr. Lima and the whiteboard while he clears his throat and orders attention from everyone. I'm one step ahead.

I'm not the sharpest student. I know that, but I always do my best. Today is going to be different. My best today means being both fast and correct. Ready for a surprise, Mr. Lima? I know I am.

Mr. Lima distributes a handout, delivering a stack of paper to the students in the front row. We're supposed to take one assignment and hand back the rest to reach the last row.

When I turn back to pass on the paper stack, I chat with Romeu, who sits behind me. He's the smartest fifth grader. And he's calm, too. We don't hang out much but do chat whenever assignments travel between us.

Today is different, though. I hand the bundle to Romeu, and I turn back right away. I hope he doesn't bug me later about it. I can't take another friend being upset with me.

My plan is to finish the assignment before anyone else. I have to nail all the answers, or I'll have to repeat them until I get them right.

"You must focus," Mr. Lima always says.

"Focus, and your potential will fly high above the sky," Dad says when I'm mad at my homework.

I do focus.

I'm an artist. I can't be in the world without watching, listening, and smelling everything. I need the big picture and the details all together. The class and the assignments are too narrow for me.

Checking on the assignment makes me hot and tired. The wrinkles on my forehead remind me of Mom's wild sea whenever she hurries. I use my hand like a tissue. I'm sweating.

I take my sweater off to breathe better (slowly, so my time can stretch out). And I straighten my glasses and curl the end of a strand of hair around my left index finger. I have to get this right.

There's this quiet noise of arms shuffling over paper and the thump of books here and there. And the squeak of chairs shifting around. And it smells like too many people thinking in a closed space, despite the door being open.

I focus so hard that I'm still sweating when I finish the assignment. During that time, the world went silent in my head. And I'm coming back with all five senses like I wanted Calvin to do. *(Please, come back. To me.)*

I lift my head and glance around. Everyone is still working. Am I the winner?

I raise my hand, and Mr. Lima comes to my desk. I hand him the assignment.

"Do you want to confirm number four?" Mr. Lima asks.

I nod my head. I don't want to, but I can't tell him that. I don't want to make Mr. Lima sad by letting him believe his students don't try. And that they don't take second chances when they come along. And I do love second chances. It's proof that time can stretch out for everyone.

I stare at the assignment on the table, defying my will. I take a deep breath.

Answering number four doesn't come as quickly as I'd like, but I'm done.

I raise my hand again. My head takes one second longer to keep up with my hand.

I realize Mr. Lima is behind me, close to Romeu. Mr. Lima puts Romeu's assignment down on his table. When I don't hear a word or any comments from Mr. Lima, I know I'm not getting the gold. It's okay, though. I'm happy for Romeu as he wins the secret competition.

Mr. Lima comes next to me and holds the sheet of paper with both hands. He smiles and puts the assignment down, resting on the desk.

"Can I help?" I ask. Today, I choose not to draw while I'm waiting.

Mr. Lima allows the fastest students to help their classmates. Of course, only if they behave, without disturbing who is working.

"Sure," Mr. Lima says. "You're brilliant when you focus, Amelia. Good job."

I'm proud and can't get the smile off my face, although I try to hide it. I don't want to show off.

Mom says humility is a good principle but not a rule.

I like principles more than rules. They're smart and soft, like a good friend watching your back.

I stand up and go around the class, searching for someone who needs help. I don't do this often because I never try to finish early.

I walk silently like the floor is ice, and I'm sliding.

I can see Iris in the back as I'm standing in the front corner of the room. I don't want to walk straight to her. My plan is working, and I don't want to ruin it.

In that short second, my eyes meet Camila's. She's staring at me like she wants to understand what I'm up to. My eyes dive down.

It's not brave. I know.

I'm not trying to be brave. I only want a friend. One that means a fresh start and talking about things besides singing and dancing.

I'm not helping Camila today, and I can't care if she's okay about it. The feeling relieves and hurts me at the same time.

I take a deep breath for the thousandth time today. I'm working on getting this right on my first attempt.

My lenses fog a bit, and I wait a few seconds before going around the room. I avoid being close to Camila. It takes more steps to get to Iris, but I have time. It stretched because of my breathing.

I keep going with my plan. I'm just about to reach Iris when I hear Luis call me on my right. I hope Iris doesn't ask Romeu for help before I finish helping Luis. But I guess not, because she doesn't know anyone. She may not be comfortable asking someone she just met about something she doesn't understand. I know I wouldn't. I don't want to risk it, though. I barely hear and see what Luis asks me. Mr. Lima notices my rush and comes to meet us to help Luis.

I take one step backward and wait. I take another. And wait again. It's as if I'm not there, invisible like a sugar apple.

It's going better than I expected, and I should be taking notes in case I need to repeat each step in the future. But before I can think of how I did it, I turn to Iris.

"Olá," I say.

"Olá," Iris says.

Her accent is different. I find it mysterious and cool.

"I'm Amelia. Do you need help?"

"I'm good," Iris says.

"I can help you with number four." I see she skipped the question.

Iris's head comes up, and she watches me, trying to guess if I'm telling the teacher she skipped the question. I smile at her. She smiles back.

I'm soft and slow with my words like I wish people were with me. I don't want others to hear my doubts. I'm sure Iris doesn't like it either.

Iris does nothing but listen. She breathes quietly, which I like. And she focuses only on the paper and my pencil.

"Do you want to try it yourself?" I ask.

Iris says nothing. She takes her pencil and writes down the answer as if I've given it to her.

Iris stares at me, and I smile at her. She smiles back.

I know she's relieved and happy. I can feel it.

"I can show you around the school during lunch break," I say.

Iris stares at me. She doesn't answer straight away, and the bubbles in my throat threaten to erupt as I freeze.

"Okay," Iris says.

The air flows out of my mouth, bringing me back to life.

"Okay," I say. "Okay."

I'm happy. And I'm feeling less lonely already.

Chapter 10

Sugar apples and chinchillas look the same. Not that they look alike, but they have a lot in common. They're both sweet on the inside and soft on the outside.

I can be like that, too. And sometimes, I can be the opposite: sour on the inside and hard on the outside.

I don't do it on purpose. It's the way my eyes appear when I'm not well. I'm happy that my light-blue glasses help hide it.

The bell rings. It's lunchtime.

I get up quickly and glance backward. Iris is still sitting. She's going through her things slowly, as if she's trying to delay leaving the classroom. It's a good plan since she doesn't know the school or anyone around.

I go to her with my closest-to-regular-as-possible walk. I don't want her to think I am desperate.

"You want to go?" I ask.

"Okay," Iris says. She stands up and smiles.

We leave the classroom together with the other fifth graders. It feels good to be with someone again, although we're still getting to know each other. And though we can't call each other friends yet.

I'm so happy. I'm sure I've grown an inch taller, and I'm floating on air like Calvin's hair when shedding from his body.

We get to the sunny corridor and walk closer to the window. It's an enormous window, floor to ceiling and wall to wall.

"Outside here is the cube," I explain to Iris.

"The cube?" Iris asks.

"Yes," I say. "The space in the middle is the cube. It's a square space, and we call it the cube. We like it there. I like the long benches where you can lie in the sun, warm and cozy."

Iris smiles like she understands what I'm thinking as well as saying.

I take her out through the cube. It's cold, but it smells like spring. The low sun shines just enough to warm us through our winter sweaters. We don't need jackets because there's no wind today, just like I thought there wouldn't be.

Boys and girls are playing soccer. We have to dance around if we don't want the ball to hit us.

Iris and I cross the cube. We hear someone shouting from one of the corners of the improvised field.

"Cuidado!" It comes loud in our direction. "Watch out!"

Iris turns around and stops the ball with her chest. It falls beautifully into her knee and left foot. She passes it over, leaving everyone's mouth open, mine included.

"That's cool," I say.

"Obigadâ," Iris says.

"You're welcome. So, you play soccer?" I ask her.

"My Papá taught me a few moves," Iris says.

"He must be a great player."

"He was," Iris says.

I'm unsure if I should ask her if her father chose not to play soccer anymore or if something else happened.

I don't want to scare Iris away by being too curious too soon.

I decide I'll ask her later when the moment is right.

Iris doesn't seem bothered that we stopped talking about soccer. She's busy checking out everything around her, filling her eyes with every inch of the playground. She must be worried about remembering every corner to find her way around whenever she's alone. For when I'm not here for her. Except that it won't happen. I won't leave Iris alone.

And I'll tell her how important she is to me as we become better friends.

"I can come with you every day," I tell her. "Don't worry about memorizing it all at once."

"Obigadâ," Iris says. She's obviously relieved.

We sit on one of the cube's benches for a few minutes.

"I've never been to Madeira," I say.

The island must explain Iris's accent.

"You'd like it there," Iris says. "I can take you on a tour someday."

"I'd love that."

I'm happy. We're friends with plans for the future. And nothing about talents and shows so far.

I can't wait to tell Calvin about Iris.

I have to ask Dad to tell me about Madeira. I'll learn everything. I'll work really hard to focus.

Mom will be so excited for her admirable daughter. I'll show her my kind-of-hidden smile for extra humility points.

Iris and I go to the lunchroom. I'm starving, and I bet Iris i, too.

Miss Paula smiles at me from the kitchen.

"How are you today, my good eater?" Miss Paula says once she meets me at the table.

We sit in the third row from the kitchen. It's where I sit every day. Camila was always next to me, but the seat's empty now. Iris takes it and keeps me company.

"Good," I say. "This is Iris. She's new here."

"Nice to meet you, Iris. Welcome to the school."

"Obigadâ," Iris says to Miss Paula.

"That's not how you say it," a small girl yells from the row behind us.

I've seen her before, but I don't know her name. She enjoys showing off by picking on everybody.

The small girl takes over the conversation, leaving no room for Miss Paula to speak to us.

"It's *ob-RRR-igad-AAA.*" The girl works hard to stress the "r" and the "a."

I see heads popping up like mushrooms. Girls and boys around raise their heads to see what's happening.

I can see that the girl is a troublemaker and doesn't respect others' privacy. But no one respects anyone's privacy apparently, because all the kids stare at Iris, which they shouldn't. They're staring at her because they don't know her. I get that. But the girl is putting on a show, although I can tell right away that she's showing off skills no one should be proud of.

Worse, the kids don't just *look* at Iris. They giggle and point at her. And they whisper in each other's ears. They're being mean, and it's wrong.

Iris is new here. She doesn't speak like the rest of us. So what?

People should want to meet her and be respectful. Instead, they're making fun of Iris.

My stomach aches more now than when I was dreading someone finding out I hid in the bathroom to skip the talent show. Even though I don't speak differently, I didn't speak at all then. Not in public, nor to Camila. And not even to my parents or Mr. Lima.

At least Iris faces her fears. Still, her face turns red like a ripe tomato, and her eyes fall to the floor.

The bubbles in my throat grow and become a roar. Why would anyone feel happy interrupting others? And just to say something that isn't nice?

I'm not comfortable talking back, but I'm getting used to being aware and acting on my own. I'm losing control like Mom and Dad lost Calvin. And I'm not finding it back.

"You're good at correcting, huh?" I shoot out into the air. My eyes don't leave the small girl. "It only means you *could* understand what she said, right? What's your problem? When did you start lecturing on proper speaking? Didn't anyone lecture you on good manners and being nice?"

It's hard to tell if she is about to cry or laugh, but the girl is working hard to hide whatever she's feeling.

I should have been softer, I guess. But people shouldn't mess around with how others speak. It's hard enough as it is for some of us. First, it takes courage to express thoughts with words loud enough for others to hear. Why would anyone ever want to say a single word? Because we have to, of course. Let us say what we want, when, and how we want. Second, count how many grammar rules there are. Did you count them all? Most are hard to figure out. It's like they're hiding. It's like stepping into a minefield every time we open our mouths. Leave us be. *Leave Iris be!*

Miss Paula isn't happy, though. She's not facing me, but her entire body twitches, telling me she's upset.

The small girl is spitting her food out after nervously choking on it. All because of what I said. But what about what she said?

Miss Paula looks at me like I should've known better.

"Be kind, Amelia," Miss Paula says.

The girl should've been kinder, too. That's what I think.

I can't tell Miss Paula that, though. That wouldn't be polite. Grown-ups tell kids whatever they want, but we kids must always behave well. Even when reason is on our side and we aren't treated with good manners in return.

I eat fast. I want to leave.

"Eat a bit more," I tell Iris. "For us to go. You can do it."

Iris stares like she can see through me. My sad face is on. But, this time, I'm actually sad. It must mean more than my words because after the silence that grows between Iris and me, she dries her eyes and starts eating. Not fast, but fast enough.

We run outside when our plates are almost empty. We try to go unnoticed despite the looks from everyone in the lunchroom.

I wasn't that good of an eater today. But I'm happier than yesterday, despite Miss Paula looking at me like she doesn't recognize me.

Chapter 11

I don't want to stay in the cube or near the lunchroom. I need to be out of everyone's sight.

I don't want to go to the basketball court either. Camila might be there with all her talented friends.

I grab Iris's hand and drag her to the open-air lobby next to the lunchroom. Her hand falls into mine, warm and soft, like we've known each other forever.

I pull her a bit longer, and we get close to the flower bed next to the school entrance. Miss Paula can't see us here.

I like this place. It smells like a wetland despite the bright sun shining today.

Pine bark covers the dark-brown dirt like a blanket.

The extract from the bark provides warmth and adds to the plants' food. Mom uses it to grow her garden, too.

Still, here and there, the dirt shows between the bark. And the lavender, honeysuckle, orchids, and camellias grow like they own the place.

Hundreds of kids kick the pine bark off the garden each day when they shouldn't be stepping on the flower bed. Sometimes the bark becomes as scarce as the lost fur on Calvin's tail.

I search for a stick.

I find two good ones near the outside wall. They're long and strong.

"Choose one," I tell Iris.

"What for?" Iris asks.

"Do you like to draw?" I ask as I start to draw a whale in the dirt using a stick.

Iris looks at me like she'd prefer to be playing soccer than drawing. Still, she's here, with a big smile, too, since we left the lunchroom.

The wet, dark dirt makes it hard to get a clear line. I can be fluid with my drawing, but here it's stuck as if the stick is giving me a fight. I feel my own stubbornness fighting in the opposite direction.

Iris laughs at my failed attempts.

Two good things come from this. One, the damp earth that gets stuck to the end of the stick allows me to draw on the cement right next to the flower bed. Two, Iris is laughing. I laugh, too.

I offer the two sticks to Iris again. She chooses the one with the dirt on the end. I take the other and dip it into the flower bed, like ink to use on the cement. We both have paint on our brushes. We're ready to draw.

"I'm drawing a chinchilla," I say.

"What's that?" Iris asks.

I can't believe Iris doesn't know what a chinchilla is! Can it be that chinchillas don't do well in Madeira? Or perhaps they're rare there. I have to find this out.

"It's the softest and nicest rodent you'll ever meet," I say.

"That's cool," Iris says. "I'd like to see one."

"I'd like to show you one," I say. My heart gets sad as the image of Calvin comes to my mind, although I keep my smile on. I choose to be happy today. "What are you doing?" I ask.

Iris appears to be drawing waves, but she scribbles all over her drawing, and I can't understand it.

"It's a mess," she says. Does she feel like a mes,s too? I can't tell.

"That's okay," I say.

I mess up my drawing so we can laugh together at our messes. And we can make more mess and laugh more.

"Olá!"

I bring my eyes up from the floor. Camila is one step away from us, standing up straight with a confident smile. I stare at her, but not a single word comes out of my mouth. Iris watches me. She's confused, and I'm sure she doesn't know what to do.

"Can I join?" Camila asks.

I stay still. I missed Camila. But the first moment I'm not missing her, she's here to remind me she left me alone. Why is she here? Did the flock lose interest?

"Olá, Camila," I say. I can't laugh anymore, and I can't smile.

"Olá," Iris says.

"I'm Camila."

Time seems to stop as Camila breaks the silence and introduces herself to Iris. I should have done that. Mom would say I'm not being polite. I don't feel polite, and there must be something good in being true to ourselves. I don't care if that means not showing good manners.

"I'm Iris." Iris introduces herself, too. So I've failed twice, now.

"You like the school so far?" Camila asks. "Did you like Mr. Lima's class?"

"It's okay," Iris answers.

It's her first day. She has taken in little information. I understand she can't express her thoughts beyond an "okay."

"Amelia and I are best friends," Camila says. "We do everything together. Can I join you?"

We didn't do everything together yesterday. Or at the talent show. And Iris can tell that we didn't do everything together today. What is Camila doing?

I'm not sure Camila and I are even best friends anymore. I never told her that. Although I feel Camila failed me, I haven't told her that, either, and I'm not sure if she feels the same. Does she really not know? She must still think I'm her friend and that we can get through any problems together.

"Well, we're not dancing or singing," I say. "So, this isn't the right game for you."

I'm upset that only now has Camila remembered I existed. At least, that's how she's behaving. My newfound confidence, coming from who-knows-where, is leaking out. I'm not sure if it's really confidence, or just anger. Still, it's showing, and not in the best way.

Camila stands in front of both Iris and me. Her smile gently goes away. I can see it disappear, like watching the sun dip below the horizon.

I've never watched Camila lose her sparkle until now. And now that I see it, I'm not sure if she ever really had it in her. Am I only now seeing the real Camila?

She's regular, like me. Her regular, wavy hair. Her normal brown skin. Her brown eyes are like mine, too. I still think she's special. But she's becoming more like a common Pokémon instead of a rare one before my eyes.

Camila's face never turns red. But now, she's medium pink. Her eyes are getting wet, and she's about to cry.

That's one thing about Camila I still find rare: Her height never changes, no matter how she's feeling. She's taller than the highest skyscraper, even when she's miserable.

"Okay," Camila says in a thin voice that sounds like a whisper.

She turns around and shuffles her feet as if she has high heels on. Except that Camila would be proud to be wearing heels. And she isn't proud right now.

I watch her go and say nothing. It's bittersweet. I care about Camila, and she shouldn't feel abandoned only because I felt abandoned by her. But maybe now Camila will understand how I felt when she left me.

I change my mind. It's all bitter, and there's no bit of sweetness!

I turn to Iris as if nothing happened. Her eyebrows raise. She's not convinced it's nothing. Worse, I don't want her to think I'm not a good friend. I don't want to be her friend just because she knows no one else.

Iris doesn't know about the talent show, or how Camila and I fell out over it. She doesn't know about me not having any talent, getting cold feet, and running away. I want it to be that way for a bit longer. I found one way to go back in time, even if it means I have to play in different spots and with new friends.

Iris says nothing about Camila and the weird conversation we just had. I won't explain, either. I don't want to talk about it. I don't want to remember everything that broke my heart. I want to move on. I like that Iris and I can talk about things that are different than what Camila and I used to talk about. And I like that we can do things that are different than what Camila and I used to do.

We stare at each other, and I smile at her, hoping my smile erases the memory of Camila from her mind.

Iris smiles back. Good feelings and fireworks flood my heart.

I can learn soccer, and Iris can learn to draw. I repeat this to myself until I believe it. We won't have anything to show onstage, but I'll be okay with that. I'll figure out what to show later. It's not too late.

Tomorrow I'll learn soccer and teach Iris more of my drawing skills.

I want Iris to have fun and be friends with me. We're becoming close already, drawing together with our sticks. We don't need anybody else.

All I need now is to figure out a plan that convinces Mom to keep Calvin's cage. I need to teach Mom and Dad how to be patient and how to stretch out time. Calvin will come home if we keep his cage and we're patient enough.

Mom and Dad can't know for sure if Calvin died. They didn't see him escape from his cage, that's why. But he's brilliant. He'll come home. He'll come home to me.

Chapter 12

Iris and I head to the cube. After the conversation with Camila, I couldn't care less if Miss Paula or anyone else saw us.

We sit on the bench. It's empty, and I'm sure nobody will come and join us. I'm working hard not to frown or cry, and I'm sure it shows.

The iron and the wood from the bench aren't warm enough, but sitting under the sun feels right. The warmth calms me down, and time stretches out again. I don't want to be the person with the throat bubbles and the dizziness.

My mind rests, but my feet hang wildly.

I could stand here, miss class, and miss dinner. Nobody would notice. Nobody but Camila, Mom, Dad, Lucas, and Mr. Lima noticed I was gone from the school's talent show.

Okay, maybe that's a lot!

If I stay quiet, I'll look like a statue. If I'm slow enough, maybe I can turn into one. And people will sit and talk about who I was.

"The best eater," they'll say. "Pity she missed the talent show. Not a dancer for sure."

"Are you okay?" Iris wakes me from my zombie state.

Staying here might not be a good idea after all. That's okay, though. I don't worry about Camila and the school anymore. I have Iris, and I'll find a way to bring Calvin home. I need to get him back, and the cage is the answer. Mom can't throw it away.

I nod at Iris while my mind travels far away from the bench we sit on.

A chinchilla's cage is where it spends most of its time—most of its life. It's its home.

The cage has to be comfortable and have all the accessories.

I can't say Calvin's cage is comfortable anymore. It's an empty white box with bars all over it. It's missing all the hiding spots where Calvin could sleep or chill and feel secure.

We still have the accessories. Mom only cleaned them and put them away.

It won't be easy to convince her to keep a big cage like Calvin's, unless I can find a good use for it.

"What would you do with a big empty cage?" I ask Iris.

It's a weird question, and Iris's face shows me precisely that.

"How big?" Iris asks either way. "And what kind of a cage?"

"A regular one," I say. "Rectangular. All white. Two stories."

"Why is it empty?" Iris asks.

"It just is." I don't want to lie to Iris, but I also don't want to explain about Calvin. "And I'd love to give it some use. Any ideas?"

I can ask Mom and Dad to get another chinchilla. That would be the easiest way to keep the cage. I can't, though. I can't replace Calvin. Not now. First, if I replaced him, it would be like saying I stopped believing he'd return. That I'm not waiting for Calvin any longer. *And* that I'm okay with it. Second, it would make Mom and Dad think that I'm okay stopping my search for Calvin. It would be like I was admitting they were right.

Having another chinchilla would be saying goodbye to Calvin—meaning I wouldn't be trying everything in my power to get him back. Or could it be a good thing? I'm not sure. Would Calvin like to have company?

I'd want to ask Calvin before assuming he'd like to share his cage with another chinchilla. What if they don't get along? What if he feels I'm replacing him? But he'd have his cage back, filled with hay and sawdust. And water and food. The cage would have all the familiar smells. Calvin could smell them from a distance and return.

"You can turn the cage into a piece of art," Iris says. "I can tell you're into art."

I'd like that. It wouldn't appeal to Calvin's senses, but at least I wouldn't be replacing him.

"I can draw and paint landscapes from the Andes," I say without realizing I'm speaking out loud.

"The Andes?" Iris asks.

"I like the Andes," I say quickly, so I don't have to go into more detail. "I'd love to go there. I can also fill it with flowers and beautiful rocks."

"You can add shells from the sea," Iris says.

The idea is clear in my mind. We can leave the cage where it is now, in Dad's office. It takes up space already, and I can make it beautiful.

People like to attach colored ribbons and padlocks to the bridge railings where I live. The bridges cross the river, and the river crosses the city, like veins keeping a giant's body alive.

The ribbons fly in the afternoon wind, and the padlocks jingle.

People make promises and take pictures as they try to attach everything securely enough to last a lifetime.

I can attach ribbons and padlocks to Calvin's cage. I can make it a real piece of art that reminds Mom and Dad of the city. And I can bring it out in spring and summer to let the breeze rattle each lock against the cage bars to create a metallic music that fills the backyard.

I can leave the cage under the shade of the sugar apple tree. And when it lets go of twenty-one more leaves, they'll work their way through the bars and find a home inside Calvin's cage.

"Or I can use the cage as a small vegetable garden," I say.

Iris's face lights up, and she smiles wide.

"You can use its base to hold the land," Iris says.

"It's big enough to grow lettuce and strawberries," I say. "And the bars will help keep the sparrows and magpies away from the seeds and seedlings."

I can make lovely things from Calvin's cage. Why would Mom give it away? I can make this work.

I don't want to ruin the cage, though—the salty air outside coats the railings and everything made of iron with rust. *I know!* After spring and summer, I'll clean everything when the air fills with humidity.

I'll move the lettuces and the strawberries to the big vegetable garden Mom cherishes under the lemon tree. I'll find space between the tomatoes, the blackberries, the passion fruit, the cabbages, the spinach, and the mint. And between the peppers and eggplants.

Mom won't let my lettuces and strawberries die.

The well-cleaned, white cage can then have space in my room.

"Or I can use it as shelves for books and decorative stuff," I say.

"That's creative, too," Iris says.

I don't have a big room, but there's always space for Calvin and his cage. I'll find the space.

The only problem is if Mom or Dad don't let me, since I'll need to move the furniture around. I can see Mom's forehead going wild in my mind—me demanding help and time from her short day.

I'll need to buy dirt and seeds. Or the ribbons and the padlocks. I'll need the space, whether inside or in the backyard.

It's not that it's complicated. It isn't. But it may be hard for Mom, since she's the one I have to convince to keep the cage. I don't want to worry her.

"I can also use the cage for an animal," I say.

It doesn't have to shelter a chinchilla. That way, I wouldn't be replacing Calvin.

It wouldn't have the same smells, of course. But it wouldn't if I used it for art, a vegetable garden, or bookshelves, either.

The thing is: I don't want a different animal. I want my Calvin.

"I don't want to buy one, though." I try to lead Iris away from the easy answer to my problem.

"Can you find someone to lend you a pet?" Iris says.

That's smart! Who would lend me a pet while I wait for Calvin?

"I can offer to babysit the neighbors' parakeets," I say. "They have their own cage, but I could use mine while cleaning theirs. I'd be offering a full service while they were on vacation."

"Wow!" Iris gets surprised. "You're starting a business."

I don't care about businesses, though. All I want is for Calvin to be back inside his cage so I can touch him again. I decide to change the subject.

"The cage can also be a temporary home for my uncle's hedgehog, Sharpy," I say.

I don't know if Sharpy lives in a cage, but in my mind, it's perfect. Sharpy's the same size as Calvin. Or was? I'm not sure how big they grow. Or if my uncle would be willing to drive and leave Sharpy with me.

"Or, I could use the cage for a turtle," I add.

Olivia has one. I don't know her well, but she lives only a few streets up.

"Turtles need ponds, though," Iris says. "Or puddles, or small swimming pools, depending on their sizes."

Calvin's cage is not prepared to hold water. But it can keep a small animal pool inside.

"Yeah, you're right," I say.

I don't know. Why should I put a pond turtle inside Calvin's cage? Turtles don't need a cage, do they?

I stretch out on the bench. I haven't moved in a while. My legs and back are numb, and I appreciate the movement.

The sun is warm enough now to give me the energy I was missing.

I bring all the ideas together and mix them in my head.

The main thing is that I can't bother Mom or Dad. But I can get help from Lucas if he doesn't realize he's helping me. Otherwise, he'll scream my plan out loud for Dad and Mom to hear before I can explain myself.

There's a turtle in Lucas's classroom. Eva is not Lucas's—true—but she's the responsibility of every kid in that class.

I take a few steps while I organize my ideas. They are mixed up like a Rubik's Cube. I've never been good at solving one of those, but I don't have to. Colors don't need to match to make it work. I only need to keep calm and bright and *breathe*.

A plan slowly forms in my head, and my heart bursts with joy. I'll put it into practice starting tomorrow.

The good thing is that Calvin's coming back home to me. The bad thing is that it doesn't depend entirely on me.

"Let's do something else," I tell Iris with renewed happiness.

While Iris and I move away from the bench, I put all my hopes into my plan. It has to work.

Chapter 13

If I sleep more, I can add years to my life. I read that some-where, and it seemed an important statement.

Sugar apple trees can grow fruit for around fifteen years. Chinchillas live between ten to twenty years. I'm ten—much less than twenty.

Calvin is twenty-one years old. He's older than any chin-chilla I know. And that's because his home was always clean, with fresh food, water, and love. And because he slept all day until I got home from school. And most of the night.

I loved waking him up to say hello, and giving him food and a sand bath, as much as I loved dancing with Camila.

I won't allow Camila or anyone else to catch me by sur-prise again. Camila would never leave the flock with all its magic and glitter, anyway.

I secretly hoped Camila would say she was sorry for leaving me all by myself. She should have told me that per-forming without me wasn't the same for her—that no one replaces me and our friendship. And that she chooses me over fame and everything else. She should want to be my friend and wish to be close to me before I found someone else to be friends with.

And I would have been ready to practice our songs at our spot again. The two of us together. Never separate. I would say yes to whatever new music she suggests.

It didn't happen that way. I'm glad I didn't hope out loud to anyone, Calvin included. It'd be embarrassing. Now, I can forget all about Camila and school to focus on bringing Calvin home.

For the rest of the day, I revisit the details of my plan in my mind. It's all in my head. I work extra hard to pay less attention to class. That's because I need to keep enough space in my brain for my plan. Each detail has to be ready and set.

It all starts with Eva. The idea sped into my head without anyone pushing me to go faster. Not even Iris.

Eva spends her days in Lucas's classroom, except for the weekends. She seems like the best red-eared slider, semi-aquatic turtle.

The sides of her head show off two red drops, like they're falling from her eyes. She's always elongating her neck because she works hard to watch what everyone's doing. At least, that's what Lucas tells us at home.

She's dark green. I want to say Eva's covered with moss, but that's not true. It might be true if she didn't spend all her time away from the portable swimming pool.

Mrs. Costa, Lucas's teacher, bought her that pool. Eva never complained or made a sound about it. Still, she keeps ignoring it whenever she feels like it.

Mrs. Costa moved Eva from the windowsill to the floor to prevent her from falling. That's why she walks around in freedom.

Lucas says Eva travels between spots of sunlight to play and rest all over the wooden floor. Eva's perfect in the way she silently stays wild.

Eva returns to the small pool to cool down and eat—the way Calvin should return to his cage. Except no one's helping Calvin now that he's lost. I wasn't there to take care of him. I'll be there for him from now on.

Each Friday, Mrs. Costa asks for a volunteer in Lucas's class to take Eva home.

"You have to volunteer for us to take care of Eva this weekend," I tell Lucas. At the same time, I stab the tablecloth with my fork. I'm careful enough not to ruin or stain the tablecloth. I know our dinner rules.

"Amelia, please keep the fork on the plate," Mom says. She's not happy. That's because Mom ignores how careful I am. "It's bad manners," she says. That's because she doesn't know how good it feels.

"Lucas, do you hear me?" I ask again, ignoring Mom. "Bring Eva home this weekend. Please. You know I love turtles."

"I can't," Lucas says.

"Why not?" I ask.

"I don't want to," Lucas shouts at me. "Okay?"

Lucas's words come spiraling through the air like wet bullets, and his face turns red. He stares at me with his dark, round brown eyes, threatening to turn into flames.

"Why not?" Mom asks.

"I don't want to tell you," Lucas answers.

"It could be fun," Dad says.

"Yes," Mom agrees. "Do you want me to talk to Mrs. Costa? Lucas, please leave your sister alone. Look at me."

There's a microscopic laser beam shooting from Lucas's eyes and burning into my forehead. Mom can't see it.

I'm in pain. But I'm fighting back with my you-can't-guess-if-I'm-being-funny-or-serious smile. I let out two loud laughs, which always makes Lucas angry. And I win. Unfortunately, Mom gets angry, too.

"Stop it, Amelia," Mom says. "Lucas, I'm here."

Lucas changes the laser's direction to Mom's forehead. Mom's forehead is a wild sea. She breathes to calm it a bit.

"Do you want me to ask Mrs. Costa to bring Eva home for the weekend?" Mom asks again.

"No," Lucas says. "We can't take care of her."

"Why not?" I ask.

Lucas switches the laser beam into my forehead again.

"Lucas, why not?" Mom changes the laser's direction again, calming Lucas down.

"Eva leaves her pool most of the time," Lucas explains. "I can only bring her home if we stay in for the weekend."

"Oh well," Mom says. "I'm sorry, you guys. You know weekends are our time to bond as a family. What do we need?"

"Family and nature," the four of us say like a synchronized choir.

It's a rule. Mom likes us to bond during outdoor activities every weekend. Dad loves it because it keeps Mom's eyes away from books and her mind away from teeth and gums.

I wasn't expecting Lucas to give me a hard time about Eva.

Lucas is usually so outgoing and relaxed. Why wouldn't he ask Mrs. Costa, despite Mom not approving of being stuck at home for the weekend? I'm surprised he thought about it.

Well, I know Mom wouldn't appreciate any of this. Although she likes animals almost as much as she likes fruits and flowers.

Eva doesn't behave according to the rules. She doesn't stay in her pool like she's supposed to. I'm glad she's wild, despite living in a classroom.

It's time to put my plan into action. I eat fast. I'm that good of an eater.

"Can I leave the table, please?" I ask.

"We haven't finished," Mom says.

"I have homework to do," I say.

Mom isn't happy. I know, I know. I must finish homework as soon as I get home, after taking a shower. First, obligation; second, celebration. It's a rule. Grown-ups do nothing but think of new ones. I can't stretch my time enough to fit them all in.

I put on my sad face. I've been watching Lucas doing it. He's an expert.

It's incredible how it always works. Most times, anyway. Enough to try it out. It helps to have big eyes, but anyone can do it. Here's how: Tilt your head to the side. Lean your ear toward your shoulder. Open your eyes wide and wrinkle your forehead a lot less than Mom does. Close your mouth and don't smile—that's a rule.

Lucas also places his hands like he's praying. That's too much for me, though. I mean, I'm ten!

"Eat some more," Mom says.

I swallow the food without chewing. I watch Mom, mouth still full. She gives me disapproving looks. I keep watching her while the food in my mouth disappears.

"Can I go now?" I ask, showing Mom a perfectly empty mouth.

"Okay, go," Mom says. "Next time—"

"I know. Next time I'll start with homework."

I fly out of my seat.

Chapter 14

"Dad, can you take the things off your desk?" I shout from Dad's office. "I need the extra space for homework."

"Amelia—" Dad says. He drags out the sound like he guesses I have something else besides homework up my sleeve.

"Please," I say before Dad finishes his sentence.

Dad meets me in his office and takes his keyboard and papers off the desk. He leaves me enough free space to work.

I sit on his chair. It's big and cozy and has wheels instead of stationary legs. I love using the lever to move the seat up and down, too. Mostly, though, I love sitting up, my legs beneath the desk's top. I could rule the world from here.

I'll have my own desk and chair with little wheels when I grow up. I'll sit high up enough to make my own rules. And when people ask me "Why?" I'll say, "It's a rule." And when people ask "Why?" again, I'll stare at them confidently and explain: "Because I say so."

Keeping the chair still is challenging, since my feet still can't reach the floor. I can manage to draw and paint like a full-grown artist, though.

I leap out of the chair onto the floor. I don't need to take another step to get to Calvin's cage. I move it away from the wall to access the back. That's where the drawings I made for Calvin still live — the only thing Mom didn't take away from Calvin's home. I pull them out from behind the bars of the cage. My heart tightens, and my arm gets stuck. I know if I ruin any of them, even if only a bit, the bubbles will grow so big in my throat that I'm sure I'll die. I'm *not* being dramatic!

The first drawing comes out. I go for numbers two and three.

My hands are tweezers. I try to be as gentle with the pictures as Calvin likes me to be with him.

I find pieces of fur still hanging from the card paper. Calvin's soft-like-home smell covers every inch of my drawings. I close my eyes as I breathe it all in. I can hear Calvin. He's here, jumping and falling around, filling in the space he left in my heart. A silent tear drops over my hand, and I awake to real life. Alone.

The three drawings are out.

I keep them under Dad's office carpet. It's sprinkled with colors, reminding me of the sweet peanut butter M&Ms, I tried once.

The drawings are safe here, hidden away from Mom's sight. I don't want her to think I'm ready to drop them in the garbage just because I took them out of the cage.

I bring my new art and exhibit it in Calvin's cage. It's awesome.

"Lucas, Mom, Dad," I call everyone into Dad's office.

"Amelia, what's wrong?" Dad asks.

"Nothing," I say. "Can you come?"

"Amelia, can you wait?" Mom says.

"No," I say.

Still, Mom, Dad, and Lucas make me wait, wait, and *wait* a bit longer. I hate when they do that.

I hear their steps.

"What?" Lucas says. He enters the office, but he sees nothing. "You need to work on focusing," Mom keeps telling me. But she never notices when to tell Lucas the same thing, like now.

Mom should work on her focus, too. I can't tell her that, though. It's a rule, one that makes no sense to me.

I take hold of Lucas's hands and guide him into the best position to appreciate the drawings. I go slowly, like I like people to do with me.

Lucas's mouth falls open. I turn my head to see Dad and Mom. They're staring at my art, and they're both smiling.

"You like them?" I ask. "There's one for the daytime. And another for the nighttime. And there's Eva with her turtle crowd."

I take a breath.

"Do you think she'll like these?" I ask. "Eva can come here. The pool fits inside the cage. She can take her walks while we take ours. We won't lose her while we spend time as a family. And we can come home earlier and spend time with her, too. She'll belong to the family during the weekend."

"You're a true artist," Dad says.

"You've got quite the talent, kiddo," Mom says.

I guess I do have talents. I still wish I had one I could show onstage. That reminds me that I have to work on new skills. And I haven't done my homework yet.

Mom won't be happy, but it's worth it if my talent can help me convince her not to give Calvin's cage away.

"Okay." Lucas smiles. "I'll ask Mrs. Costa to bring Eva home for the weekend."

I smile back. We all do. I love our family when we all smile together. I loved it more when Calvin smiled too.

"Your plan worked like a well-played scam," Dad would say. I think he'd be right.

"Thank you, Lucas," Mom says. "Thank you for reconsidering. And thank you, Amelia. It's sweet of you to find a way to include a pet friend in the family."

Lucas and I both smile big, proud smiles.

"What about homework, Amelia?" Mom asks.

I should see it coming.

"Give me a sec," I say.

Mom gives me a look—the sea on her forehead in full force.

"I mean, now," I say. "Trust me, Mamã."

Dad and Lucas leave the office. Lucas doesn't stop chatting about Eva and how great it will be to have her with us.

"Did you know that turtles' shells work as shields?" Lucas asks Dad. "And did you know Eva only eats three pieces of food a day? And did you know we'll have to clean her water?"

Dad leaves with a tired sigh. "Uh-huh" is the only sound he can fit between Lucas's endless enthusiasm.

The chatting fades as they walk away.

Mom stands in the office, staring at me like she's had it with me.

"Please," I say.

Mom leaves me alone. I'm not sure if she left or is eavesdropping in the hall to make sure I keep my word. I make more noise than I need to with the books and pencil on Dad's desk to convince her.

I have a short text to read and three questions to answer. I'm not sure about my third answer, but I don't ask Mom about it. I also don't give my writing a second read today. I trust it's good enough. I have to run to find my talent, still.

I close the book and put the pencil back in the pencil case. All my stuff goes into my backpack, which is ready with everything I need for tomorrow.

I head upstairs.

"Amelia!" Mom calls from down the staircase.

"All done," I shout from Mom and Dad's room.

"Do you need help with any of the homework?" Mom asks.

"No," I answer.

"Are you sure?"

"Sure, sure," I say.

I stay close to the door, one foot stepping into the hall-way and the other inside Mom and Dad's bedroom. Mom's interrogation stops, allowing me to think of other things, like talents to show onstage.

I take a deep breath.

I want to try gymnastics.

I was good when I was in elementary school. I did the handstand, the bridge, and the cartwheel. I did the hand-stand, fell into a bridge, and got up again. With no help! I want to try these again.

I go for a handstand. I don't feel secure enough to do it without something supporting my feet.

I find an empty wall in the room and start. It's going pretty well. I do it a few times before I hear Mom ask me from downstairs what I am doing. She *could* come up and see for herself!

"Nothing," I answer. "It's a handstand."

"A handstand?" Mom says. I can tell from her voice that she's surprised. "After dinner?"

"Yes," I say. "I'm good."

Mom says nothing for a short second.

"Where are you doing that?" Mom asks.

"In your room."

"Yes, but where?" Mom insists.

"Against the wall."

"The white wall?" Mom says. "Do you want to leave spots all over the wall? Stop that."

I thought Mom would be pleased that I was carefully doing the handstand against a wall. I try against the closet. My feet knocking on the doors makes a loud sound.

"Amelia!" Mom says from downstairs.

"I'm doing it against the closet doors," I shout.

"Stop that," Mom says. "It's too noisy."

I stop the handstand and work on my cartwheel instead.

It goes well, but it's not perfect. Before I can try one more, Mom walks up the stairs. Her steps are strong and sound like a storm that's about to burst.

I stop what I'm doing and speed to my room.

I sit on my bed with a book in my hands, open where the bookmark waits.

Mom goes from her room to mine. She opens the door and stares at me. The stormy sea on her forehead proves I'm right about her mood.

"I'm done," I say.

"Good," Mom says. She's not happy.

Mom leaves my bedroom, and I stand there reading my book like I'm blind. I can't sound out a single line.

I can't do gymnastics in school. I need to be good before I show off. It's bad enough that I failed the talent show. And so far, I haven't been able to get up to improve my cooking. I knew I wouldn't. I'm not good at anything. This is not going well. The days are running, and I have nothing.

My heart jumps in my chest, and tears flood my eyes. I swallow them and all the feelings that come with them.

I stay there, alone in my bed, pretending I'm reading when all I'm doing is trying to think of a talent I can show in school.

Chapter 15

I wake to the sound of nothing. The light that shines through the window blind is dim.

I reach my hand outside the blankets into the cold and grab my glasses and my watch.

Lying in bed, I work hard to adjust my eyesight to the few lights that force entry into the room. When I can see the clock's hands, I plant my head deep back into my pillow.

It's early. I can sleep longer, or I can think of fresh new talents. I choose the latter.

I could get up now and practice my dancing again. Or the handstand or the bridge. But I'm warm and comfortable under the covers and don't feel like getting up. Also, the noise would wake everyone up. Mom or Dad may be awake already, but Lucas might complain. I don't want to deal with any trouble.

I hear the cracks and snaps of the wood floor breaking through the morning silence.

I didn't use to like the noises that crack and snap everywhere around the house. I remember thinking about ghosts or intruders wandering invisible—all hidden—right before I peeked into the hall or empty rooms.

I like the sounds now. They remind me of Calvin. I close my eyes, and it's like I can hear him downstairs in Dad's office inside his cage.

The cracks and snaps are getting louder. Mom or Dad wakes up and goes down the stairs.

I should get up, get ready, and hurry to the kitchen to work on my cooking skills. I *should*. But I don't feel like learning anything from Mom today. She didn't help me much yesterday.

Still, it's already Thursday. I need to hurry about finding my talent.

I remember Lucas's book of magic. Learning tricks seems like a good deal.

Lucas keeps the book in his room, on the shelf near his bedside table. It's a bad idea to go in there, but it's the only idea I have right now.

I stretch as much as possible, letting every inch of warmth that spreads along the mattress touch my body.

I fold the blanket down over my waist, inviting the cold in.

One foot at a time, I push the rest of the blanket down to the bottom of the bed.

I sit on the edge of the bed and get up, ready to take one step forward. The floor erupts with noises under my foot. That's the problem with old houses. Some things will always be old and cranky, just like this floor that complains in every possible way.

I sit on the floor and drag my bottom with the help of both feet and hands. There's still noise, but much less.

I drag myself like I'm trying to get rid of a terrible itch until I reach the hall. At the sight of no one, I keep pulling until I arrive at Lucas's bedroom and slide the door soundlessly in the air.

I hear Lucas breathing and feel the tired air leaving the room. My heart beats fast once I reach for the shelf beside Lucas's bed. It's loud, and it may wake him. But Lucas stays still, the air leaving softly through his mouth and nose and going inside again.

When I take the book in my hands, the sugar apple tree comes to mind. I try to shake it off as it becomes so vivid. The tree stands tall, resting against the soft wind, the leaves falling in a single spot near its trunk.

The sugar apple tree fills a void in my head like ghosts fill the hole of the night. I stay still, meditating, working to give the vision meaning. But as soon as it comes, it's gone.

I turn around, bottom still on the floor, and get ready to head back out to the hall. The book stays stuck between my knees. I squeeze them together hard. I don't want the book to land on the floor and wake Lucas up.

I should have asked Lucas, I know. But I have no time and no choice. It's a matter of talent or shame for the rest of the school year.

Lucas moves in bed to fall into a new position, and I wait to see if he wakes up. He turns again, dragging my attention and the book, which slides quickly down to the ground before I grab it with my feet.

Sweat drips over my face and arms. A pond is opening under me, and I'm drowning in it.

I stay there, quiet and motionless, staring at Lucas like I'm stealing his most precious belonging from a room filled with laser alarms.

Lucas doesn't move, and I get my bottom moving back to my room. My feet and hands are red when I get there. My heart feels odd, and my head pounds. I feel like resting, but I have to put my hands to work.

I go through the book's pages with images showing each trick's steps. My eyes travel through the text for extra detail.

Most tricks are too complicated: too many steps or too much text. Some I don't like, or they need extra material I don't have.

Magic is tricky, but I push the thought away and try a simple illusion.

I take the magic wand from inside the book in my right hand. It's black, with two white ends, and not too long.

I'm supposed to hold it between my thumb and fore-finger and wave it in the air. And I'm supposed to watch it bend despite being stiff. It should be easy. The picture in the book explains how simple it is.

I wave it in front of me, and nothing. I can only see a silly stick moving in the air. I move my fingers closer to the end of the wand and try again. I work on different waving techniques until I find one that fills me with hope. Yes, it bends. It's an illusion, but it bends. It's cool.

I open the wardrobe door to watch this in front of the mirror and repeat each step. The wand doesn't bend.

I run my hands along the wand to see if I ruined it. No, it's the same. Why doesn't it bend anymore?

I try again and again. Nothing.

I try one last time. I shake the wand in the air, forcing it to bend. It doesn't.

I have both hands at the white ends now. *Bend, wand. Bend!*

The crack comes louder than the sounds the old pine floor makes.

I have two wands now, one edge in each hand. I stare at them. My hands, my whole self. I'm disappointed by this dull wand that refused to bend. Magic is definitely not for me.

I hear someone coming. Mom or Dad must have heard the wand cracking.

I slide the book under my bed, take off my glasses, turn down the light, and lie still. Two broken wands under my pillow. I pull the covers up to my neck and close my eyes.

I see nothing but Lucas's face crying. He'll be sad once he knows I broke his wand. He'll be disappointed with me. I can't bear having Lucas feel like that because of me.

Lucas will miss the book the moment he wakes up. Right now, I want nothing else with talents.

The steps reach the top of the staircase and stop.

My heart goes so crazy inside my chest that I hold both hands open over it, which I don't think will really work to quiet it down.

My head is filled with thoughts of Lucas and how he was so happy when he got the magic book and saw the wand and all the accessories.

It's only a wand, but it's his. And I had to ruin it.

The image travels every inch of my mind, making me confused and dizzy. I dig into the mattress like it's as soft and empty as a cloud—until the thin, last layer of the cloud breaks into bare space, and I fall. And fall. And keep falling, working hard to grab onto something but it's all air.

My eyes open against the salty sweat draining from my forehead and onto my eyelashes. I'm not falling anymore, although my stomach did drop against my spine at full speed.

I push the blanket down with both feet to get the cold air to dry my soaked pajamas.

I fell asleep. Was it a dream?

My hands automatically reach under the pillow. It wasn't a dream. It's the sad reality. The two broken ends of the wand in my hands show me I shouldn't expect anything good coming out of this week.

I bring the half-wands close to my chest and then throw them under the bed, next to the book and my will to be someone else. And I bury it all together with pain and I-don't-have-a-clue-how-to-fix-this dust powder.

Lucas may never bring Eva home once he finds out about the wand. And I'll lose the cage forever.

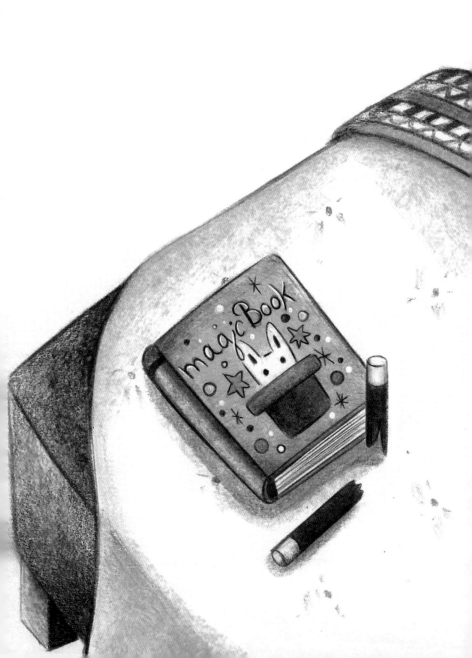

Chapter 16

Sugar apples and chinchillas are good at hiding, like spies on a secret mission.

Sugar apples hide behind the leaves. I can spot them when they sway in the wind, but I have to be vigilant and search hard. My glasses are often in the way when I try to look up.

I want sugar apples to teach me to be here but not be noticed. I'd like to be invisible sometimes.

I don't think of it as a talent. It's a superpower.

Chinchillas hide from confusion, loud noises, and new smells. It all triggers their alert system, and there they go. They disappear into hiding places away from sight and danger. Or simply to rest.

I must have found one of the best hiding spots ever. I don't forget the wand, broken into two sad pieces hidden under my bed. And I can't believe Lucas acted all normal this morning, mentioning nothing about the book.

One of two things must be true. Lucas saw the book was missing and decided to wait for the best time to tell Mom. Or Lucas didn't notice it, and he will go crazy when he does.

I'd like to have a secret hiding place myself. But mostly, I want Calvin to stop hiding. I want him here with me. So I can throw this feeling that pulls my stomach against my ribs under my bed as well.

Still, I keep opening up to Calvin, and my words disappear into the void. I'm sure he's listening wherever he is.

"Today was a good day if I don't think about breaking Lucas's magic wand," I tell Calvin. "And yesterday as well. As long as I don't think about Camila showing up and asking to join Iris and me. Where was she when I was alone? Will *you* only come to me if you see me with another pet?"

I shake my head to push the thought away.

I don't want another pet. And I'm sure Calvin is not like that. He loves me no matter what.

I'm sitting on the floor in Dad's home office. My back's against Calvin's cage. If I close my eyes and breathe calmly, I can feel Calvin nibbling on my hair gently.

"It was awkward, and I don't want it to happen again," I continue. "That doesn't mean I don't want to be friends with Camila anymore. It's that—I'm teaching Iris to be my friend. And I can't risk Camila coming and pulling us like mosquitoes into her light. She'll want us to sing and dance again. And I bet Iris will be the best singer, and Camila's already the best dancer. And I'm not the best at anything, so I'll have to go and make a new friend. Again."

Talking about Camila reminds me that I have no talents.

I open my eyes. The daylight runs away from the room, and the streetlights take up their space. I hear a sound coming from the door. I stay quiet, trying to figure out what it is.

My eyes shut. The night comes in and hugs me into its sadness and tiredness. Even though the windows are closed and the heat is on, there's a breeze in the room.

Behind the darkness of my closed eyes, I see sugar apple leaves dancing to the sound of the wind. I hear them humming a sad song. I'm staring from the floor, watching the leaves sing and dance. And I'm watching the branches. They embrace me like two gigantic arms, but I'm not afraid. They rock me in the air like I'm a small child. As they do, I get sadder and more tired and heavy. I'm heavy. And the branches open, and everything disappears below me. I lose everything but my weight. And I fall and fall.

I wake up before hitting the ground or being lost in the unknown. I can hardly breathe as my heart jumps up in my throat. I lean forward because I need to throw up. The feeling passes when I can control the air coming and leaving my mouth, nose, and lungs. I stay calm—the air going in and out, as slow as the waves in low tide.

My eyes and mouth are round and open as I suck all the air in.

The week is ending, and I haven't decided what talent I can show off. The thought stays with me like a close and uncomfortable hug.

I want to prove to everyone that I belong in a talent show as much as everybody else.

My breathing speeds up again. I close my eyes to calm down.

I remember the noise. It's nothing. It's only me here and the memory of Calvin getting stronger while I speak to him.

I keep going.

"I figured out how to keep your cage, Calvin," I say as I release a sigh. "Mom can't give the cage away. You'll need it when you return. Lucas must have asked Mrs. Costa today if Eva could come and visit us for the weekend. Don't you worry, okay? She's not replacing you. She's a visitor. If we treat Eva well and she comes often, there's a chance Mom won't give away the cage. Eva will only use it until you come back. But you should get your things done and find your way back fast. Please. My plan may not work for the whole school year."

I hear another sound at the door. It's too real for me to ignore it this time.

"Lucas?" I ask, trying to figure out who's making the noise.

"What's up, kiddo?" Mom comes into Dad's office.

I knew I had heard something.

"Mamá?" I ask.

"It's me," Mom says. "Are you okay?"

"I am," I say. "Why?"

Did she find Lucas's wand under my bed?

"I thought I heard you talking," Mom says. "What was it?"

"Hmm—nothing."

"Can I sit here?" Mom asks.

Before I answer, Mom sits right next to me.

"We haven't talked," Mom says. "How was your day?"

She did find the wand.

"Good."

"Good like good, or good like great?"

"It was okay," I clarify.

"That's nice," Mom says. "How's Camila?"

Okay, Mom knows nothing about the wand. This means that Lucas knows nothing yet. He hasn't missed the book on the shelf. And I still have time to figure out how to fix it.

"Camila's been busy with dancing and performing," I say. I don't feel like talking about Camila. Mom doesn't know that, and I don't want to explain why not. Mom doesn't have to know I'm not hanging out with Camila anymore.

I change the subject.

"There's a new girl in my class," I say. "Her name's Iris."

"Iris." Mom stretches the sound of the name like she's savoring the word. "That's a good name."

A smile opens in my mouth.

"And she's a good friend," I say. "Or at least that's what I feel. We're getting to know each other. She's drawing. I'm teaching her about that and how we can draw together. And I'm teaching Iris about the school, Mr. Lima, and the class."

Mom's listening and staring ahead—her forehead's a vast and calm sea.

I stop talking, and we stay silent.

I look at Mom, and her eyes travel to meet mine. I don't remember Mom having time to listen. Not without hurrying up because of dinner, baths, work, or whatever grown-ups always have to do.

I watch Mom, and she watches me. She keeps quiet and calm, like the sea on her forehead.

Mom doesn't ask questions and looks like she's really listening. Like I have all the time to say what I have to say. As if the silence can stretch beyond the room. Like it matters.

My eyes wander to the window. The yellow light that pierces through the panes covers us like a blanket.

Mom keeps staring at me like there's nothing more important to do. Her breathing is close to my hair and neck. I lean toward her.

I want to stop time and be here—the idea of Calvin behind me. And Mom by my side. No time or hurries. Just being.

I know Mom expects me to talk to her, though. She doesn't know how to be too quiet or still for too long.

"I like Iris," I say. "I think we can be friends."

I close my eyes. Mom smells like fresh orange juice, although there have been more hours than I can count since her hands squeezed the oranges in the juicer.

Orange from the oranges. Yellow from the streetlights. And green from the sugar apple tree sleeping under the cold outside. Orange, yellow, and green. And gray from Calvin's fur. A beautiful rainbow. The colors travel in my mind. And out of the blue, I'm lying back against the grass. I'm under the mixed shade of the orange and sugar apple trees. I'm lying on the floor, Camila is waiting for me at school, and Calvin is waiting for me in his cage. I can stand up and go to them. I can go back in time—when everything was like it should be.

My heart is beating like there's nothing but love around me. But Mom starts speaking.

My heart, mind, and I—as a whole—expect Mom to be here with me and not think about what comes ahead. In the end, I find that people are what they are.

I love Mom, and I love Camila. I like them as they are. So, why does it hurt?

I'm looking forward to hearing what Mom has to say. I missed spending time with her. But as the words come out of Mom's mouth, the colors of my rainbow vanish, and my world collapses.

Chapter 17

"I found a pet clinic for exotic animals," Mom says. Her voice brings me back to Dad's office when there's no Camila or Calvin. "It's close to the fire station and next to Mrs. Fonte's. They treat chinchillas."

"Like my Calvin?"

"Yes, sweetie. Like our Calvin."

"Will they come here to help us find Calvin?" I ask Mom. That is all I can think of.

"No, sweetie," Mom says. "We've talked about that. Calvin died."

"I never saw him dead."

"I know that," Mom says. "I'm starting to think I should have shown you. Dad and me—we thought we were protecting Lucas and you. You're too young. You're a child. My child."

"Did you call the pet clinic to be sure Calvin died?" I ask.

"Well, no."

"How can you be sure?" I ask.

"I'm sure, Amelia," Mom says. "Me and Dad both. We're sure. You have to trust us. I can't change that."

I frown, but Mom ignores it. We're right back where we've been since Calvin's been gone. Mom hurries to get on with anything she wants to say or do. And I pull her back. Or at least that's how I feel. We're never moving at the same pace.

"Anyway, the clinic. . ." Mom keeps going. "They appreciate all the help they can get. I don't have much free time. You know that."

Yes, I know that.

"But we should give back to the community," Mom says. "In fact, I offered to give Calvin's cage away. It can house chinchillas in recovery or waiting for a new home. I know you prepared the cage for Eva, honey. But don't you worry. I've found the perfect spot to hang your drawings for Eva to watch and feel welcome."

My dream comes back to me again. Except that now I'm awake.

I go deaf as the sugar apple branches let me fall into an empty, silent void.

Mom keeps on explaining about the perfect spot. "On the floor," she says. I can't hear her. "Not alone," she keeps going. I want her to stop. "Stay home." No. No. *No.*

My head's still lying over Mom's shoulder, but I'm not resting. I've lost myself there. A hard rock hit me and broke me. I can't think, and I can't move. I'm trapped on the shoulder of the person who will give away my friend's home. My Calvin. All I have is this cage. All I have to make sure he'll return to me.

Mom's voice echoes far away like it's coming from outside the window, behind the glass and the thick night.

She runs her hand through my hair.

The weight of my head is too much for Mom because she struggles to lift it off of her. She uses her hand, the one petting my hair, and works on pushing it. Twice.

Mom's breathing goes heavier, like my head. Like, she thinks I'm making it heavy on purpose.

My head isn't heavy. It's gone like Mom and Dad say Calvin is. It's numb. But Mom keeps ignoring that fact, pushing it with both hands, bringing me back to reality. She gives it a last hard try.

My head is up, but the feeling slips through my entire body. My head is up, but I'm numb.

"Let's have dinner, sweetie," Mom says. "It's already late."

Mom never forgets about time. I guess life goes on no matter how I'm feeling.

Mom stands up and leaves the office.

I somehow show up at the dinner table. I can't remember how or when. I'm unable to think or feel.

People keep talking around me. It's like I'm not here. I'm numb — I've turned into a sugar apple, and that's what Calvin is now, too. We're two sugar apples who did not recognize each other while hanging on the same tree. And we're waiting to fall and spend the rest of our lives apart.

People keep talking. I want them to be quiet.

I want to run to my room and be alone and quiet. But I can't because that's not good manners. Because there's a rule. And because I'm numb, I can't shout at everyone to be quiet. *Please be quiet.*

"Eva is not coming," Lucas says.

"Why?" Mom asks.

"Mrs. Costa promised Leo he could take Eva home," Lucas answers. "Mrs. Costa keeps her promises. Like we all should do. That's what she said."

"Well," Mom says. "Next time. We'll find a solution to welcome Eva when your turn comes, Lucas. I'll take good care of Amelia's drawings until then."

I hear Mom, Lucas, and Dad as I see their mouths opening and closing while they talk and eat. The movement doesn't fit the sound. Like they're in speed mode. Or in slow mode. I can't tell. I'm getting sick. The bubbles in my throat grow bigger. I'm suffocating. I open my mouth but breathe through my nose. And right when I think I'm going to die here, there's a sound erupting from my heart. It goes through the bubbles and comes to my mouth with hurry and rage, catching everyone off guard. Me included.

"Stop!"

Mom, Lucas, and Dad stop. They silence their voices. But their eyes are still loud, drilling through my brain, trying to figure out where that came from.

They're searching in the wrong place. It didn't come from my brain. There's nothing there but an empty hole where reason should live.

"Calvin's cage stays," I keep shouting. "It has to stay. Nobody is giving it away." I lower my voice. It's tiny now, and I can barely hear myself. "What if he comes back?"

"Honey," Mom says like she's drowning me and teaching me how to swim at the same time. "Calvin's not coming back."

"You don't know that," I say. I lose all the strength to shout and to look at my family. My eyes fall to my plate.

"Calvin will always live in our hearts," Mom insists. "But he's not coming back to his cage. It can host other chinchillas, though. Do you want us to think about having another one? Do you want to think about it, sweetie? We can't keep this big of an empty cage. It needs to have a use, but we can try something different. What do you think?"

"No!" I still don't shout, but my voice comes thick like mud. "You were distracted. Calvin isn't gone. I can't replace him. I'll never replace him."

I sob hard, and my lungs hurt. Still, I keep going.

"He ran away when you weren't paying attention," I say.

"No, buddy," Dad says. "We held him in our hands. It's sad, but there's nothing we can do."

"No," I insist. "I didn't hold Calvin. I didn't see him like that. He ran away when you were feeding him. You opened the cage's door, and you turned away. You can't be sure, and I don't want another chinchilla. I want Calvin. He'll come back. He needs a place to come back to. He would never leave without saying goodbye. He wouldn't leave without telling me goodbye. What if I decided to leave home? What would you do? Forget all about me and give my stuff away? Move on? Would you give my room away? Wouldn't you wait for me? What would you do? What would you do?"

My dish's full of tears. It's so full of tears that there's a lake forming, and I'm watching my face in that mirror—my sad, crying face. I want to see nothing.

I push my chair back, hard, making more noise than I'm allowed to. I'm breaking more rules than I can count.

Now my pants are wet from the tears, and I can't breathe or speak. Mom, Dad, Lucas—no one says a single word. I wanted them quiet. But now I'm not quiet. I'm a whirlwind of thoughts and fears. I have no more questions and no more words.

I get up, my head still hanging down. I stand there like I'm onstage. A stage I don't want to be on.

I watch the three people sitting before me. This is not my whole family. Calvin's missing. One of us is missing, and the rest of my family doesn't care to search further. To wait further. They gave up on him. I watch the three of them like I don't belong with them. I don't belong here.

I run through the door and march up the stairs, my knees hitting my ribs as I go.

I slam my bedroom door and land on my bed, facedown. I'm all down. I cry. And after I do, there's silence. Forever silence. No more room for questions and thoughts, and feelings.

I'm tired, and I let the dark from the room come over me. It comes inside, and I calm down. I sob. I forget. Finally, I fall asleep.

Chapter 18

Some sugar apples are heart-shaped, just like a chinchilla sleeping with its head tucked down by its belly.

They're silent, discreet, and they warm my heart.

Sugar apples and chinchillas come from far away, but they've been with me for as long as I can remember. We belong together.

"It's time, sweetie." Mom sits next to me as if nothing has changed. "Wake up."

It's morning. My mouth is dry, and it tastes like dust. I keep my lips closed and feel the inside of my mouth with my tongue.

My head pushes against the pillow. My eyelids are stuck closed.

Both my head and body hurt. I try to stretch, but I can't. I won't while Mom's here. I move an inch, hoping she can't tell I'm alive. I survived, but the pain is still here with me.

"It's Friday," Mom insists. "C'mon, honey. We'll all get to rest tomorrow."

I want to stay home, in my bed. It feels harder to ask Mom than to keep doing what I always do.

I'm like a robot, and Mom has all of the control. I'm an excellent robot because I don't speak, I don't question, and I don't argue. I do what I'm told to do. All my strength goes to doing—not talking or thinking. I'm empty.

Mom leaves the bedroom, and I sit up straight. My back and neck hurt. I stand up and take all the steps down the hallway to the bathroom.

My feet ache against the floor like old rubber bands about to burst. It hurts from my heels to the tips of my toes.

I wash my face. My head is heavy, so I have to hold it with my left hand. I use my right hand to splash water in my eyes. The cold hits my skin like tiny needles.

I decide the towel is going to do the rest of the work. It will have to do for today. I use it to wipe the stickiness out of my eyes. And I leave it there, outside the towel rail, resting on the sink. Mom never mentioned a rule against this, although I'm sure she'll make one, and I'm already breaking it.

I put my clothes on like I'm on automatic pilot. I'm a good robot.

I walk downstairs. My feet still hurt, so I must move slowly like an old lady.

I should go straight into the kitchen to give my good morning kisses. And to the table to have my breakfast. I'm not hungry. I go to Dad's office instead.

It's odd to be here. Calvin's cage is on my left. Mom hasn't given it away yet. It feels like I'm seeing it for the first time, although the drawings I made for Eva are still hanging in the back.

It's old and new at the same time. Old, since it has been my happy place for so long—I can't think of another one. New, because I can't recognize it without the hay, the straw, the wooden house, the rocks, and drawings. Without Calvin. It feels too white and too empty—too much of nothing.

I go back to the kitchen, passing Mom. She grabs my arm and holds me close. She breathes close to my ear.

"Amo-te," Mom says. "Good morning."

I know Mom loves me, but I don't feel lovable today.

Her breath is warm and smells like oranges.

I say nothing. I stand there, my hands falling on the side of my body. I give Mom time. Mine's gone.

When Mom stands tall, I move to the table. My feet still hurt inside the socks like I'm walking on knives.

I sit at the table.

I take one bite of the bread and leave the rest on the plate.

I take one sip of the milk and leave the rest in the mug.

I take one sip of the orange juice and leave the rest in the glass.

And I'm done. I'm a good robot.

Mom is either happy or doesn't notice, because she says nothing and leaves me be.

The silence eats at my voice and eyes. It opens its big mouth to swallow my entire body, skin, and soul together.

All is quiet inside of me.

I bring my things outside, my backpack and Crocs. My steps are slow and heavy, pulled by gravity with more anger than other days. I have to hold onto the wall not to fall. Once I get down the steps, I take the everyday walk to the mudroom. But after three or four steps, I stop.

The weight of my bag increases. I have to stick my hands below the backpack straps to stop the shoulder pain. The load is so heavy that I pull the straps off and let the backpack fall on the ground like a big rock.

I stretch to relieve the pain, my arms straight with hands clasped behind my back. I open my eyes and look up, then close them immediately. I shrink to the ground to protect myself from the very real branches that fall seemingly out of nowhere.

The adrenaline I lost invades my heart and mind in seconds and brings me back to life.

Two twigs stand before me, down on the ground. The sugar apple tree scared me, but it also gave me these two perfect twigs. One is long and thin, with both ends precisely sharpened. The second one is shorter and heavier, with light-brown flattened ends.

I take both sticks and put them inside my bag.

I test the backpack's weight with my hands. Up and down. It's lighter despite the extra load!

The backpack fits nicely on my shoulders.

I stay there, watching the sugar apple tree over me for a few seconds.

"Morning," I say.

The tree says nothing but the twigs in my bag feel like enough greeting already.

I turn back and quickly head back inside. Dad and Lucas are by the door, ready to leave.

"Amelia?" Dad's surprised.

"I'm going alone today," I say.

"Going where?" Mom asks from the kitchen.

"School," I say.

"Why?" Mom asks as she comes to meet us at the door.

"I'm ten," I say. "Trust me."

I look straight into Mom's eyes and don't smile. She stares at me, but I don't think she feels defied like she sometimes does. The calm sea on her forehead tells me it's different this time. I'm different this time.

Mom looks at Dad and nods yes.

"Okay," Dad says.

Mom smiles at me, but I can't smile back.

"Be careful, honey," Mom says.

"I know." I don't look back.

I hurry my steps like I learned from Mom. I want to be alone in the mudroom and put on my sneakers without hearing or talking to anyone.

I hear Dad and Lucas chatting as they approach, but I'm ready.

I still have to wait for Dad to unlock the doors so I can get to the street.

On the sidewalk, I kiss Dad and Lucas goodbye. I give Lucas a small hug and a low whisper to his shoulder, hoping he can't hear me.

"Desculpa," I tell him. "I'll fix your wand."

Lucas is more concerned about getting rid of my hug and hears nothing. He laughs an embarrassed laugh.

"Amo-te," I whisper, already one step away from Lucas. I love Lucas, and I'm sorry for letting him down.

Dad smiles at me and takes Lucas by the hand.

I move ahead with rhythmic steps. My head is full and empty at the same time. I broke Lucas's wand. And I have no talents.

I'll never get a new wand for my brother. And I'll never find a talent to show in school.

The week is over, and all my plans are, too. I couldn't convince Mom and Dad to keep Calvin's cage. What does that say about me?

I hear a door opening behind me while my mind switches on and off.

I check over my shoulder. Mom is peeking out from behind the door. Her wide, round eyes tell me she's surprised to see me there, staring back at her.

"Making sure you have everything," Mom says. She must have wanted to go unnoticed.

"All good," I say and keep walking.

I walk on the sidewalk until I get to the music school. I turn right and go up the street. When I get close to my school, I turn back before I turn left.

I can see Mom hiding behind the bushes by the corner down the street.

I stand there, watching her. People go by me, but I keep staring.

Mom leaves the bushes to wave goodbye and give me a thumbs-up. She has an embarrassed but wide smile. I give her a shy thumbs-up and take the curve where I know Mom can't see me.

I'm almost to school, and Mom won't walk further. And I won't look back again because if I do, I'll run down the street and up the stairs to fall back into my bed and forget about the worst week of my life.

Chapter 19

I walk around the school wall until I reach the gate. It stands tall in front of me, iron painted in dark green like the ones that open wide into big villas.

I stand outside under the overhang that covers the sidewalk to protect from rain. Fathers, mothers, grandparents, and all kinds of grown-up people leave children at the school gate. And some come alone, most of them older than me.

I'm not excited, or sad, or anything about coming to school alone. I suppose I should celebrate it as a milestone because I'm becoming more mature like I'm supposed to. But I don't feel grown up or mature. I'm only watching the world running in front of me. My time has stopped, even though it seems to be moving forward for everyone else.

I'm here, but I'm not here. My heart is missing. And I have to find it. I must figure out where I lost it and bring it back, like I should have done with Calvin.

I hear a group of people approaching behind me. It's just two moms and three kids, but their voices' energy turns them into a crowd. I see them as a crowd that passes me and allows me to disappear. Behind the group, I'm invisible.

I don't think twice. I don't want to leave, but I also don't want to go inside. And I can't stand here.

I turn my back and leave the school's gate behind. The bubbles in my throat grow, but I swallow them as my glasses fog up. I have to glance down underneath my lenses. I stare at the sidewalk as my sneakers take the path in front of me like I'm not wearing them. Like they're not mine.

I'm going around the building to the right—away from home and school.

I walk as fast as I can, taking steady steps, and I don't look back. I can't risk someone recognizing me while I walk outside the school when I should be heading inside. I don't know what to say or feel, and I can't think about it either.

I walk and walk farther away, never looking back. My eyes watch my feet, one ahead of the other.

My heart hurts, and I can't hold two tears from dropping down to my light jeans. The backpack warms my back. Holding on to the straps feels like I'm carrying someone's hand in mine, and my heart hurts a bit less.

After turning left at the indoor public swimming pool, I walk up the street to the fire station square. It's a large square with four big sycamore trees. Their shadows spread around a playground with a slide that runs through the body of a giant red ant. I loved to play here when I was younger, but the place doesn't speak to me much now, especially today. All I want is to be invisible as I'm crossing it, protected from everyone's sight.

I cross the playground and pass the firefighter statue. It stands taller than everything else on the left side of the square. I take the crosswalk to the other side of the road.

It's rush hour, and people are living their everyday lives—busy with time and thoughts. I'm extra careful before crossing.

I breathe fast as I get to the other side. My breath goes in and out, in and out, working to find its rhythm.

Underneath my jacket, I'm sweating like I've run a marathon. I have to stop for a few minutes. I pause to tell myself that I can do this.

You've got this, Amelia.

I'm alert, and the muscles from every inch of my body tense up. And it's not because of the traffic, crowds, and busy living around me; it's the bubbles in my throat, again. They're back and have spread like waterfalls, filling the tips of my nails and hair. It's impossible to shake off the numbness I woke up with this morning.

I shouldn't be here now, and alone, but I can't show it. It's done, and I can't go back. Time is a one-way street, whether we go fast or slow. But my mind travels back to Monday, and I live on the girls bathroom floor again.

I start walking again. I'm going slower now, peeking through each store window before reaching Mrs. Fonte's store at number twenty-five.

Every shop here is narrow, deep, and dark. They grow inside old buildings like dead-end tunnels. It's hard to see anything unless you're already inside.

I enter Mrs. Fonte's grocery shop. She's distracted, tidying tuna cans on the shelf behind the counter.

"Good morning, Mrs. Fonte," I say in my most polite voice.

"Oh, olá Amelia," Mrs. Fonte says while turning my way. "Do you need something?"

A round face and pink cheeks frame Mrs. Fonte's warm smile. It brings her cheeks up, hiding her small black eyes behind them.

Mrs. Fonte is wearing a light blue apron, the same color as my glasses. It's tight, and she looks like she's about to burst.

I stare at Mrs. Fonte's hands and notice how she rubs them on the apron as she talks to me.

"Don't you have school today?" Mrs. Fonte asks.

"I do." I better tell the truth. "But I'm searching for a pet clinic close by. It's supposed to be for animals like chinchillas and other rodents. We're giving a cage away."

"Like for exotic animals?" Mrs. Fonte asks.

"I guess," I say. "I mean, yes." I have to sound sure.

"It's kind of you to donate your cage," Mrs. Fonte says, making me swallow the dry dust stuck in my throat. "I haven't heard about any clinic, though."

My heart falls to the floor, next to some lettuce leaves under the vegetable rack.

"But why don't you ask two doors down?" Mrs. Fonte adds. "I don't know about a pet clinic, people have been moving in and out, and it may be what you're looking for."

"Obrigada," I say. "I will."

I turn to leave the store.

"Wait," Mrs. Fonte says.

The bubbles leave the tips of my nails and hair and rush to my cheeks.

"Tell your mom I'll have peaches from our farm this weekend." Mrs. Fonte rubs her hands, again, leaving permanent wrinkles on her apron. "Have her call today if she wants me to save her some."

"I will," I say.

I don't smile or wave goodbye. I don't wish her a lovely weekend as Mom taught me. I don't want to give her time to ask me questions. Also, I'm in a hurry. I have to find the clinic.

I turn to the door and leave the grocery shop, turning right.

Eight steps ahead, I'm in front of 21 Manuel Firmino Street. The door is half open. It has six small, dusted windows, four rectangular in the middle and two square ones at the top of the door. The old wood shows beneath the chipping red paint.

I knock on the door and wait.

I knock again, this time twice. The door opens a bit with the sound of a high-pitched wheeze, but no one comes.

I persist, knocking on the left of the lower window. Knocking on the glass sounds louder than the wood. Still, no one shows up or answers from inside the building.

"Olá," I say while peeking inside.

Nothing.

"Olá," I say again, this time louder. "Anyone there?"

I knock on the glass again.

The silence inside greets me. It pulls me into a new world, despite all the rush and noises from the street.

I step one foot inside. And another. My feet drag me along with a will of their own through the narrow hall.

The strength in my legs fades a bit more each time one of them decides to take a step forward, but I keep going. It's a long hallway, and I can't see behind the inside door.

I reach the end of the hallway and press on the door slowly while I lean forward to peek my head inside. I'm shaking so hard I'm sure it's making noise, and anybody can hear it.

My left ear reaches the door first, and my right hand reaches out, fingers first and palm second. All my muscles work to push the door open. My movements fight against the rust my scared heart throws at the door hinges.

There's no way nobody hears me. My hands, arms, and shoulders down to my knees are shaking like the sugar apple branches on windy days. I listen to them myself.

My eyes adjust to the darkness inside the room that opens before me. The silence inside takes on its own sound, like when my house is quiet, and I can hear Calvin speeding around in his cage.

I'm becoming more fluid in my movements—hand, arm, and door turning into one. And then the loudest sound and the biggest pain—*WHACK!*

The door hits me hard on my forehead—a blow I don't see coming. And from one second to the next, I see, hear, and feel nothing. Blackness surrounds me.

Chapter 20

"Amelia, wake up," I hear a sound coming from far behind the blackness. The sound gets louder, bit by bit.

I force my eyes open, but they fight to stay closed. When I win the fight, my eyes take time to adjust to the light and images that form before me.

"Where am I?" My mouth moves lazily and sounds like it's full. "Who are you?"

"Amelia, it's me, Iris," the voice on the other end answers.

"Iris?" I open and close my eyes to make sense of what's happening. "How? Why? When?"

There's a hand on my shoulder that comforts and pressures me all at once.

"I followed you, okay?" the voice says, trembling like it's about to cry. "I didn't want to go to school without you. I'm not sure I like it there, but I like you."

The image in front of me becomes clear, and I see Iris standing over me, her hand resting on my shoulder. I move my eyes around her to understand where I am and if we're alone. The room is white and bright from the light of the rectangular lamp on the ceiling. There's no one else there besides Iris.

"I saw you leaving, and I followed behind." Iris sighs. "I called you a few times, but not loud enough. You didn't hear me. I couldn't go back. I didn't know what to do. We just met, and I didn't want you to think I was stalking you or anything."

Iris speaks fast, like a speed train that you see one minute and is gone the next. I'm dizzy and need to focus on understanding what she's telling me.

"Wait," I say. "What?"

"I decided to wait behind you," Iris says, slowly this time. "I figured you'd head back to school, and I could follow. I don't know the streets and the places. I couldn't go back alone."

Iris is stumbling on her words, and she starts to cry a little.

"I can't skip—you know," Iris hesitates, lowering her voice and watching the door. "My mom—you know."

I don't know. I'm lying on a doctor's bed. I move to sit, and my head hurts.

"Easy there," someone says.

I didn't realize someone had entered the room while I was trying to sit up. I watch the lady dressed in pale green scrubs with light green eyes behind colorless glasses. She's standing next to Iris, who's red-faced and teary.

"I'm Bela," the lady introduces herself. "Dr. B."

"Desculpe," I apologize. "I'm Amelia. Where am I?"

"You're at my clinic," Dr. B says. "I didn't see you behind the door and slammed it into your face. I'm sorry for that. You fell from the hit. And I guess from the fright? Are you feeling better now?"

"I am," I say. "Desculpe. I knocked and called, but I heard no answer. I should have waited."

I take my hand to the spot on my forehead that hurts.

"We had ice on your forehead," Dr. B says. "Do you need more?"

"I'm good," I say, taking both legs to the edge of the bed, "I—I mean, we have to go back. I wanted to visit the clinic if there was any."

"There is," Dr. B says. "Or there will be. We're getting everything ready to open soon."

"Will you treat chinchillas here?" I ask.

"We will. Chinchillas and all kinds of exotic animals. We left flyers at the fire station for people to know us and help if they can."

"Mamá told me," I say.

"That's good news," Dr. B says. "We're getting noticed."

"Mamá says you need cages."

"We do, Amelia. We appreciate donations as we're starting out."

"Can you do it?" I ask.

"Do what?" Dr. B says.

"Can you treat animals like chinchillas?"

"We can," Dr. B says. "It depends on what each animal needs, but exotic pet clinics have success stories we're proud of."

"My chinchilla is twenty-one years old," I say.

I eye Dr. B from my sitting spot on the bed to watch for her reaction.

"Is that so?" Dr. B is surprised but confident. "You must be proud. You have a tough fellow there." She hesitates, and her expression becomes more serious. "You must also prepare yourself. Your friend may not last much longer."

My eyes search deeply into Dr. B's, trying a spell that prevents her from talking. I tell her nothing, though. I can only sound out a sigh.

"Be happy, Amelia," Dr. B says. "I'm sure you shared many great moments with your chinchilla, and it's time you can give your love to another one. And who knows? You may still have a little time ahead with this good, old friend."

I'm not happy, and I don't want another chinchilla. Also, I don't have time for this, and Iris stares at me in despair.

"We have to go," I say, taking a slight leap out of bed. "Obrigada," I thank Dr. B.

I have to leave this place. I want to go because of Iris but also because I don't want to hear about losing Calvin.

Dr. B is real, the clinic is real, and everything else makes sense in the real world, where time still flows. But not in my world.

"You're welcome," Dr. B says. "And I'm sorry. Again. Do you need me to call your parents?"

"Não," both Iris and I say at the exact same time. We can't risk anyone calling our parents.

"Obrigada," I say, trying to disguise any concerns she may notice. "Mrs. Fonte from the grocery already called them," I lie. "Mamã is coming there to pick us up." I hate lying, but I couldn't think of anything else to say.

"You can visit another day," Dr. B says. "I can show you around. Bring your mom to visit, too."

"I will." I won't.

"You, too, Iris," Dr. B adds.

"Okay, adeus," we hurry to say goodbye.

Iris and I head outside. We take all the steps we need to get far away from Dr. B's clinic and Mrs. Fonte's grocery shop. We walk side by side in silence. Iris's head is down. She's staring at the ground.

"Are you okay?" I ask Iris.

Iris drags her eyes from the ground and smiles at me while she nods yes.

"Are you okay?" Iris asks me.

"I'm not sure," I say.

"Your head." Iris looks at my forehead. "I know."

"It's not my head." I stare down as my mind goes through the entire week's events. I must look odd because Iris asks me nothing else.

"Come on," I say, staring forward after what feels like forever. "Let's go back to school."

"Sorry for coming after you," Iris says before we start moving.

"Não," I say. "Don't be sorry. Thank you for not leaving me alone."

Iris takes my hand as she stands in front of me and squeezes it to let me know she's also not alone when she's with me. My body relaxes like I'm being hugged.

I look at Iris.

"Ready to run?" I ask.

Iris nods, and we run as fast as we can. Our backpacks dance on our backs, and our legs bend behind us. And our squeezed hands move back and forth, back and forth. We run the whole way back to school, and I don't think about being invisible anymore.

The school's iron gate is closed when we reach it, which means classes have started.

The watch on my left wrist tells me we're late, but not *that* late. We still have time to catch up on Mr. Lima's class.

I think about what I'll tell Mr. Lima about being late. And about being with Iris. A thousand ideas come to my mind, and I work fast to organize them into the closest-to-the-truth explanation.

I reach my finger out to press the doorbell, but it goes over someone else's. My hand flies away to my back, and I turn to see who arrived first.

Camila stands beside me, her forefinger pressing the doorbell and waiting for someone to answer. I want to say something, but nothing comes out of my round mouth, holding my chin hung in surprise.

"Sim?" the janitor says.

"It's Camila from Mr. Lima's class," Camila says. "I had a doctor's appointment. Can I go inside, please?"

Iris and I stand next to Camila in silence. Camila stares straight through the gate like we're not there.

"I can't get over there right now," the janitor says. "I'll open the gate from here. Please, make sure it's closed before heading to class, okay?"

"Okay," Camila says.

The mechanical sound of the gate opening tells Camila she can step inside. Iris and I stay outside, not sure what to do. We don't have any reasonable explanation for the janitor to let us in.

Camila pushes the gate in and holds it with her hand, arm stretched to give us space.

"Are you coming?" Camila asks.

"But—" Nothing else comes out of my mouth.

Camila doesn't leave before we get through.

"Obrigada," I say as we move inside.

The three of us go in and give it a hard push to make sure the gate closes. The loud sound of the iron clapping tells us it's safe.

As we run to the classroom, I can only think how nice it is of Camila to let us in. And that Iris must have a thousand questions for me. I have a few myself. Right now, I clear all the questions, fears, and fog from my mind and try to walk as fast as I can.

Chapter 21

Camila, Iris, and I arrive at the door to our class. It's open like always, Mr. Lima's voice wafting out into the hall.

Camila knocks on the door the minute we arrive, and Mr. Lima welcomes her in. She disguises a short peek at Iris and me once she steps inside. And like nothing happened, Camila keeps walking toward her seat.

I take a few seconds before deciding what to do next. Iris stands beside me, waiting for a reaction.

I hear Mr. Lima talking to Romeu about his assignment, the one about talents and the talent show. I couldn't care less about that dumb show. It's Friday, and I don't have any talent that shows others I'm good at something. I couldn't learn a skill in time for today. I wanted to tell everyone it was okay, that I didn't mind missing the talent show. I could tell my class that I had figured out what I was good at and could show it to them. I could prove it. But not anymore.

I breathe before holding my closed fist in the air, ready to knock before entering.

When I'm about to knock, Iris grabs my other hand with both of hers, her eyes closed like she's praying.

"Are you okay?" I ask.

Iris nods yes and releases my hand. I can tell something is worrying her.

"Are you ready?" I ask.

"Ready," Iris says, freeing a deep sigh from her mouth. It stays open after freeing the air out.

I knock on the classroom's door with three short knocks.

The entire class stares back at us. My skin burns like it's the middle of summer and I've scalded my face. I can't tell how Iris is doing. I can't turn my head. I can only face forward, where Mr. Lima stands tall, close to the whiteboard.

"Girls," Mr. Lima says. "Is everything okay? I had no notes from your parents informing me you'd be late."

"Desculpe, Mr. Lima," I say. I want him to know we're sorry.

Iris stays silent.

"We're fine," I continue. "We—"

"Not now, Amelia," Mr. Lima interrupts me.

His face and tone show me he's irritated that we interrupted the class. I don't care, though. I'd hate to talk in front of everyone.

"We'll talk at the end of the class," Mr. Lima adds. "Take your seats, please."

Iris goes straight to her seat at the back row, while I have to pass all the rows to get to my seat near the whiteboard. It's the first time I don't think this is the best seat in the classroom.

I try to be quiet. It's impossible to do anything right with all eyes set on me. People stare at me from the moment I enter the classroom until I take my backpack off and sit at my desk. Mr. Lima waits in silence until I'm ready to pay attention, making me more nervous by calling all the attention to me.

I don't know about Iris, but I'm starting to think that being on a stage isn't for me. I'm not sure I like to be the center of even this tiny universe, much less the entire school.

Mr. Lima clears his voice and resumes the class. He forgot what he was telling Romeu, and I can see that it upsets him more than it should. He stops, recovering his posture, and focuses on a different student.

Iris and I haven't missed much. Iris came to our class after we had already written the assignment. And there's nothing to discuss about my assignment. I don't have any talent and wasn't part of the talent show. We should be excused from the class altogether instead of having to justify arriving late.

Mr. Lima ends up not talking to me about my assignment. I was lucky, or he's upset. I can't tell.

He teaches the rest of the class with his usual enthusiasm. Yet, this time, it feels like a circus. I'm not into juggling today.

I'm not into learning, listening, or engaging in any way. I'm losing myself inside these walls.

I spend the class staring outside while the lecture goes on in front of me.

All I hear is people talking. The sounds enter my ears like they're coming to me underwater. It's slow and distant and sad and away.

Mr. Lima asks no questions today. At least he asks me none.

The clock hands go around and around. Come together. Stay apart. Together. Apart. They don't give up on each other. I know that, although I continue to stare outside.

The bell rings. I notice my eyes hurt. It must be from not blinking enough.

I put both my hands on my desk to lift me. My chair slides only when my body stands straight, making it noisier than it should be.

I feel Mr. Lima's eyes burning on me. We're supposed to have manners and not make noise. But I run out of strength, and I turn into the robot again. I don't look at him. My eyes fall to the floor like they're attracted to wood and dirt from pencils and erasers. I look up to watch Iris in the back row. We both stand, waiting for everyone to leave the classroom before speaking with Mr. Lima.

The noise is high and endless. It takes forever to get stuff off of desks, trade opinions about everything, and forget something somewhere.

While everyone and every sound works their way out of the room, I visit the ideas in my mind. I gathered a few to explain why we arrived late. I had them organized in my head. But they're gone—like Calvin's gone.

I think I have a problem with keeping things. I'm losing everything lately.

The room finally goes silent, but my mind is not.

Think, Amelia. Please. What's wrong with me?

I'm still standing and staring at the back of the classroom. Iris is staring at me, her eyes asking silent questions about what she should do now.

Mr. Lima clears his throat. The sound comes from his desk behind me.

I glance at him and smile a small smile.

"So, can you please approach?" And he clears his throat again. "Both of you."

Iris timidly walks to the front row. I wait for her before walking the walk that separates me from the front of the classroom.

Mr. Lima's desk stands between us, until he leaves his seat and sits over the table to be closer and taller. I'm not sure if he wants to look us in the eyes or show he's the boss. Or both.

"Do you want to tell me what happened?" he asks.

Silence fills every inch of the room. You could hear a pin drop. A group of kids runs on the outside, and we listen to their laughs. It's easier to have noise from the outside.

I look at Iris, and she stares back at me. Her eyes ask me to say something.

"Desculpe," I say. "We're sorry for arriving late without notice."

Mr. Lima keeps staring, waiting for me to say more than simply apologize.

"It's that—"

"Amelia, breathe," Mr. Lima says. His body relaxes as he sits at the table. "Whatever it was, you can tell me. Are you both okay?"

"We are," I say.

"Okay, good," Mr. Lima says. "Now breathe and tell me what happened. The truth, please."

I go through all the ideas in my head. They feel like a tangle of loose sentences that don't fit together. The truth? I don't know.

I take a deep breath, close my eyes, and decide the truth is the way to go. Nothing worse can happen. I've already lost Calvin and Camila. I lost my spot at the talent show, and I'm about to lose Lucas's confidence when he realizes I broke his magic wand. And worse, I've lost myself. I have no talents and can't learn any, either.

"I visited a pet clinic for exotic animals near the fire station." My words come fast. I don't need time to think this through and regret them. "I asked Iris to come with me. She didn't want to come."

Okay, I don't have to tell the *whole* truth. Why should Iris take any blame? She's new here. That's all she needs.

"Is that true?" Mr. Lima asks.

I nod yes with such power that I don't leave space for Iris to say anything else or for Mr. Lima to doubt my words.

"The clinic is opening soon, and they're asking for volunteers to donate time or stuff," I continue. "My mom told me she can't give away her time, but she wants us to donate our chinchilla's cage."

My chest tightens as I'm talking about Calvin and giving away his cage. The pain is unbearable, but I have to speak now. I don't like talking about things that make me feel sad. Mr. Lima knows it. I wrote about it in my assignment. I don't like it, but I have no other choice. Mr. Lima is giving me no other option.

"We went to check on the clinic," I say. "I wanted to make sure they would put the cage to good use. It's important to me."

"Why is it so important that it couldn't wait for Saturday?" Mr. Lima asks. "Couldn't you go tomorrow?"

The truth about Mr. Lima's words takes me to a place where I can't explain myself and only wish I hadn't said a single word. Except that now, I can't run away.

Chapter 22

The bubbles in my throat feel like they're about to reach the boiling point.

"Desculpe," I say. The word comes out clumsily, but Mr. Lima must know I'm sorry. I stay quiet for a few seconds. "You're right," I finish.

Mr. Lima's body relaxes again. His shoulders are lower, and his cheeks are softer than I have ever seen them. He's not acting like a boss, and he's not angry. He's listening.

I'm done. I've explained everything, and Mr. Lima doesn't make weird faces at my explanation, making me think he's okay with it. I don't want to remember this week or talk about it anymore. That's why I can't explain why I keep talking.

"Calvin's missing," I say out of the blue.

"Calvin?" Mr. Lima asks, and I'm sure Iris is asking the same question in silence.

"My chinchilla," I say. "Calvin is twenty-one years old."

"I'm sorry to hear that," Mr. Lima says.

"Mamã is giving Calvin's cage away, and I couldn't wait for tomorrow." My words come out like sobs. "And I'm sorry. I had to make sure. I had to know they'd take good care of it. You know, to help—other chinchillas."

Mr. Lima sighs. I don't think my reason is good enough for him. But I think he accepts it as a good enough reason for me.

"I'm glad you're moving on," Mr. Lima says. "And I'm happy you've found a friend who moves on with you."

I don't want to move on. Not without Calvin. But it's true. I found Iris in the middle of losing a lot this week.

"Now, I'll have to report the incident to your parents," Mr. Lima adds.

"Please don't." It's the only sentence Iris speaks.

"I'll tell you what," Mr. Lima says. "I'll give you a head start and speak to your parents on Monday. That way, you have time for your own version during the weekend. It's my best and final offer."

Iris and I nod our heads up and down in agreement. We have no other choice.

Arriving late at school is the third strike after missing the talent show and breaking Lucas's wand. I suspect I'll be grounded for life.

"Now, about the assignment," Mr. Lima adds.

I shrink inside, thinking we're discussing what I wrote out loud, but the bell rings louder, and I stare at Mr. Lima like I'm ready to leave.

"You're off the hook, Amelia," Mr. Lima says. "For now. Don't miss class or be late again without your parents alerting me. And, before leaving—"

My body melts on the floor in front of him.

"One last thing," Mr. Lima adds. "Most talents don't show on top of a stage. I understand you'd love to make others forget. That would be easy."

My hands move behind my back, and my eyes fall down to my feet. *Please, stop.*

"I'm glad that you make others remember, instead," Mr. Lima concludes.

What does he mean? I'm not glad if people remember my failure at the talent show.

"Now, off you go." Mr. Lima sends us away.

Iris and I step out into the corridor, ready for the lunch break. We walk to the cube outside and sit in silence on the closest bench. The kids at school celebrate any free time like crazy, stretching out and jumping around. Backpacks get strewn all over the floor.

We had enough excitement for today.

The sun warms my entire face. The kids from each grade run, bounce, laugh, and shout. There's life everywhere I turn. It's loud with colors and smells. I want to feel like that again. I want to shake off the grays and the dust.

"I failed the talent show right before you joined our class." Why am I speaking? "Camila went on without me," I keep going. "I have no talents."

I don't know what's happening today. I can't stop my mouth from speaking and my stomach from turning. I skipped breakfast, so I must be hungry now.

"That's not true," Iris says.

"Why?"

"I saw you drawing," Iris says. "You're good. You have talents."

"Yes, but—" I'm sure Iris doesn't know about true talents. "I mean, I can't dance, sing, or play anything good enough to show it onstage."

"Why would you want that?"

"To be part of the talent show, of course," I answer.

"Why don't you offer to draw and paint the background scene for the stage?"

My gray and dust vanish away.

"That's smart," I don't want to sound *too* enthusiastic. "It's there the entire show. People would know I did that."

"And they'd remember," Iris winks at me and sighs like she wants to add more. "You don't like to remember? Or be remembered?"

"I do," I say. Why is Iris asking me this?

"Mr. Lima said you want to forget," Iris says. "Or you want to make people forget."

I think I look like I don't want to talk anymore because I don't. Iris hesitates. But she sits up straight and keeps going, ignoring whatever face I'm making.

"I like to remember," Iris says. "I'll always remember you stood up for me in the lunchroom, and just now with Mr. Lima. Thank you for that." Iris smiles at me and looks forward like she's getting ready for takeoff. "I'll always remember my dad. He's dead."

I take Iris's hand in mine. Her eyes are wide open.

"I'm sorry to hear that." My words sound low. "I didn't mean it like that," I try to explain. "I want others to forget asking me about things. Sad things."

"Why?" Iris asks.

"It makes me sadder." I also stare straight ahead. "And—I don't know. Saying things out loud might make them come true."

Iris and I sit staring at the horizon and watching nothing. My eyes hurt.

"You can't change that," Iris says, bringing me back to her.

"What?" I ask.

"You know, my dad died. Not saying it out loud won't bring him back to life. It's not less true if I shut things inside."

"Yes, but you saw him, right? You went to the funeral."

Iris nods like I sound foolish.

"My parents say Calvin died, but I never saw him." I sound hurt. "I shouldn't be telling you this. Your father died. It's not the same. Desculpa."

Now Iris wrinkles her face and stares at me like she expects me to continue.

"My chinchilla was there in the morning and gone when I got home." I stare at Iris, eyes wide open. "I never kissed Calvin goodbye. He was small, gray, and quiet. Still, he was family to me. My best friend."

"Obigadâ," Iris says. "You know—for sharing."

My eyes fall to my lap. I'm hungry and tired.

"How did you survive that?" I ask. "I mean, I feel like I'm dying inside."

"You don't." Iris looks the most serious I've ever seen her. "But talking helps. Talking to you helps me."

My hands go to my face, but then I let them fall on my lap. All my confusion melts together.

Sadness gains roots and grows if we keep it inside.

Maybe we're supposed to talk about it. To set it free.

Maybe when sad feelings travel to the head, they shrink to fit the path inside the body. And they keep getting smaller to travel to the mouth and turn into sound. And vanish on their way out.

Or maybe sad feelings don't disappear. They stay with us for life. But if we share them a bit at a time, we can be happy despite remembering what made us sad in the beginning. As time passes and we talk things out, emotions take up less space in our hearts.

My voice fights the rust in my throat and finds its way out.

"I've been keeping track of the bubbles in my throat," I say.

"What?" Iris asks.

"It happens all the time," I keep going. "It's like I have this bubble thing in my throat. Bubbles come and go. I think they're like gates. You know, like the school gate. The bubbles in my throat keep sad things inside. And they grow and rot there. I keep storing sad things inside my heart. I guess if we free up our hearts—" I stop. "If we can keep spare space in our hearts, we can welcome Calvin and your dad back home whenever they want. Although we can't see them, they can still come back to us."

Iris puts her arm over my back and lays her head on it, like an odd hug. Her voice sounds so close to my back that it enters through the sweater and my skin underneath.

"Papá used to care about how I say things," Iris says.

"Mamã worries about how Lucas says things, too," I say.

"Lucas?"

"My brother," I say.

"I used to go to speech therapy," Iris says.

"Lucas goes to speech therapy," I say. "Not everyone understands him when he talks fast. I do. I make sure I hear him as if he's speaking slowly when he goes fast. I'll never make him sad by not listening or not understanding."

"You understand me, too," Iris says.

I nod yes. I do understand.

"I'll talk to Mamã at home," I say. "She'll talk to the speech therapist to help you."

The sun feels like a blanket around Iris and me.

I'm not at home. I'm not at Dad's office, and still, I'm not alone. I'm not standing against Calvin's cage and I am still alive. I'm sad, but it doesn't hurt as much anymore.

Iris and I smile. I'm pink and light—and starving.

Chapter 23

Iris stands up, and then I stand up. We're warm inside and out. We take the few steps that lead to the lunchroom.

We take our seats after grabbing our food. My eyes meet Miss Paula's far back in the kitchen. She nods to me, and I nod back and smile. Miss Paula smiles back.

I eat fast, but in silence. Iris eats slowly. She stays quiet, too, but I think her mind is speaking a lot inside. That's the only reason I can think of for Iris to eat that slowly. It's okay, though. I like slow. I can wait.

Iris finishes eating. I finished a while ago.

We both stand up and go outside, close to the flower bed where we hid our sticks the other day, to keep practicing our dirt drawings. They're visible but well disguised, like the sugar apples. We left them on the ground, over a spot with dark-brown land, the same color as the sticks. They were close to the wall, where no one passed. Nobody noticed them, even though they were in plain sight for everyone to see.

"Wait," I say.

With the stick in her hand, Iris stands up straight, ready to listen.

"Would you rather play soccer?" I ask. "I can talk to Romeu for you to play with them."

Iris's smile opens. It's the best idea I've had since she's met me.

"Will you play with us?" Iris asks.

My eyes look right and left, right and left, like there's no chance I'll ever play soccer. Much less with the boys.

"I'm terrible at soccer," I say. "I will ruin the game. But you can go. You're great. I can cheer."

"I'd love that," Iris says. My heart sinks. "But not today. Today we draw. Can you teach me? Next week, I'll teach you to kick the ball."

"It sounds like a plan," I say, feeling better already. "A good one."

We take our sticks and get ready to start drawing. That's when I hear another voice.

"Olá," Camila says.

"Olá," I say.

"Olá," Iris says.

"Can I join you?" Camila asks.

She stands in front of Iris and me. She's not tall or sparkling today. The Camila I know is there, and I've missed her.

"Sure," I say.

Iris smiles.

"Here, have my stick," I say. "Dip it into the dirt to draw better. I'll find one for me."

I stretch my arm out with my stick tight in my hand. Camila reaches out and holds it in her hand. She doesn't give it a second thought. That's one thing I love about Camila: She's determined.

Camila and Iris wait for me to find a stick.

I search everywhere in the flower bed. A few sticks rest under the lavender but are weak and break when I press them onto the cement ground to draw. I find a strong one close to the honeysuckle, but it's too short.

Camila and Iris are talking while my search to find something to draw goes nowhere. How come when I need something it disappears from the face of the earth? Or at least from my school and this flower bed, flooded with sticks, rocks, and whatever else we needed two days ago? Now, nothing. At least nothing good enough to work.

I stretch my back up straight. It's aching from bending over to find a good-enough stick.

I hold both hands behind my back and stretch my arms. It feels good.

My hands fall next to my legs, and a deep sigh leaves my nose. What will I do?

My mind switches when I stuff my hands in my pockets. Where is the sugar apple leaf? I had it just the other day. It helped me feel better.

Wait—*the sugar apple tree!*

My heart pounds, my mind brightens, and my feet gain new life and speed.

"Hey! Where are you—" Camila and Iris try to ask, but I'm one step ahead.

"Give me a sec." My words drag behind my rushed sneakers. I'm fast.

I knock three short knocks at the classroom door. No one's inside but Mr. Lima, making it much easier to feel at ease.

"Olá, Amelia," Mr. Lima says.

"I need something from my bag," I say. "Can I come in?"

"Sure," Mr. Lima says. "Take your time."

I find my backpack in a pile of fifth-grade bags. I move a few to the side to see mine below. I forgot I put the sugar apple twigs in here. I should have been more careful.

The zipper slides opens, and I wait to see both twigs broken into small pieces of sugar apple wood. But they're both still whole, each of them a single piece.

I smile and take the big twig out—the one with the sharp ends. I take it with both hands and hold it close to my heart. This was a beautiful present.

I find a safe place inside my bag for the shorter twig. I don't want it to break, and it won't snap between the books. I know exactly how I'll use it.

I close the zipper and leave my backpack where it was, straighter and tidier this time.

"Obrigada," I thank Mr. Lima while flying out the door without giving him time to say something back.

When I get back to Camila and Iris, they start to use their sticks. They scratch them against the floor, but they're doing less than a few lines. An,d well, I can't tell how the lines work together or what they're drawing.

I show them my perfect twig, holding it proudly in my hand. There is a huge smile on my face I can't hide. I don't care if that shows no humility on my part.

But I don't want to draw and show off my talent. I want to have fun with my friends.

"Can you teach us your moves?" I ask Camila. "We can dance while we draw."

Camila's smile opens big. She turns pink and sparkling. Another thing I like about Camila: She's an instant star.

I grab a big chunk of dirt with my perfect twig. I take it to the cement and write, "I'm sorry about your dad." I draw a heart and a house close to it. The stick flows smoothly like a pencil.

Iris sees my sentence while drawing. She stares at me and says nothing.

Iris comes close with her stick and writes under my sentence. "I'm sorry about Calvin." And she draws a heart and a house like I did. That's because she knows Calvin and her dad live in our hearts.

I smile. It's a small smile, but it's not sad.

Camila comes close to us. She grabs her stick and lots of dirt. She writes, "I'm sorry." She draws nothing, not only because she can't tell why we're drawing a heart and a house, but also because she can't draw. And that's okay. She can still hang out with us.

I drop the stick on the cement floor and jump up to hug Camila. Iris jumps, too, and hugs us both. And as we stand there hugging each other, I want time to slow down and stretch as much as possible.

The air smells warm, like the sea and spring together, all mixed with lavender, honeysuckle, orchids, and camellias.

It's still cold, but I can see swallows flying overhead and resting high on the electrical wires. A flock of flamingos cuts the blue from the sky like fast clouds. One's lost, but I believe it'll find its way to meet the flock—like Camila found her way back to me.

We're dancing and drawing at our new spot.

We don't need a stage. We can use all our talents and use all the cement to be artists or whatever we want to be. And to communicate better and be true friends.

The bell rings, and we head back into the classroom.

Camila and Iris leave their sticks in the flower bed in the same spot where we left them yesterday. I keep mine with me. It's dirty, and anyone who sees it will think I'm crazy, but I don't care.

I hide the twig under my sweater. I don't want Mr. Lima to tell me to leave it outside the classroom. I'll put it in my bag as soon as I have it.

My sweater will get dirty inside, and my books may get messy. But this was a gift, and despite it meaning nothing to others, it is special to me, no matter how much dirt it brings.

I can't help staring outside while the afternoon class goes on in front of me. I can't focus today, and I guess Mr. Lima can't, either. He never tells me to pay attention. It must be a fascinating topic for him, as he keeps talking, and talking, and smiles, and asks only a few questions.

I'll pay attention next week. Today, I need the sun to keep the dark away.

Chapter 24

When I get home after school, I go straight to my bedroom.

I forget to wash my hands. Okay, I don't forget about that, but I don't want to be near Dad's office and find out the cage is gone.

The door to my room is closed, which never happens. Mom says spaces need to breathe, and the door is their nose. We need to keep doors open. It's a rule!

I open it to find Calvin's cage in the center of the room. I go around it. The drawings I made for Eva are gone. Instead, I find the ones I made for Calvin when I was tiny, long ago. Someone took them from under Dad's office carpet.

There's an envelope lying inside the cage. My eyes missed it at first because the cage's bottom is so white without the hay and everything. And the envelope is white as well.

I open the white, barred door and take the envelope out. I open it carefully because I don't want to tear it.

Inside the envelope, I find a picture of Calvin. My Calvin! There's a small piece of paper with a note. I recognize Mom's handwriting.

"Here's to second chances. Calvin loved you with all his heart. You were and will always be home to him. Let him rest in peace. I hope you find the space and time to say goodbye and find the best way to honor his place. Love, Mom, Dad, Lucas."

I love when Mom talks to me and I can understand her. I love second chances.

My eyes blur, and the lenses of my light-blue glasses fog.

I realize Mom's leaning against the door to my room. I know it's her by the way she stands there with her arms crossed like she's the boss here. I know she's making an effort to give me time and not speak right away. I'm starting to get my space as a sub-boss myself. I'm the boss of my room and the boss of my time. That's enough for now.

I keep staring at the picture and the note until I make sure my eyes can see again. I make sure my lenses are dry and clear again. I want to be able to see Mom once I face her.

"Olá, Mamã," I say as I stand and turn to her. I keep holding the envelope with the picture and the paper note.

"Olá, Amelia," Mom says. "Are you feeling better?"

"I am."

"That's good to hear," Mom says. "Did you have a nice day at school?"

"I did."

I take a few steps closer to Mom and hold her hand.

I guide her to sit on the floor. I sit right in front of her, with my face turned away.

"Iris misses her dad," I say. "He's gone, and now she left home to come here, and she'll never get to have the smells and feel his things again."

Mom keeps silent.

I can't see her. I lean my back against her chest.

Mom's breath is calm, and she smells like oranges.

I use both my hands to find Mom's hands. I guide them to my hair.

"Take small strands," I say. "Small, quiet strands."

Mom does precisely what I ask her without arguing. I guess this can be a rule between us. I talk, and Mom caresses my hair. I like this rule, and I can see how useful it can be to have some rules after all. It opens the way to communicate. We know what we're supposed to do without asking for it all the time.

"Iris talked to me about her dad," I keep saying. "Her heart feels better now. She has space there to remember him forever."

Mom's hands move slowly over my hair. I get goose bumps.

"She used to go to speech therapy," I say. "You know, like Lucas. You may want to talk to Lucass' speech therapist for her to help Iris. Will you?"

"Sure, sweetie," Mom says.

"I went to visit the pet clinic today," I say. "The one you're giving Calvin's cage to."

"I know," Mom says. I wasn't expecting to hear that. My eyes dive down into the carpet. "I was behind you all the way until you got back to school."

"I wanted to make sure they were there, like you said," I say. "And they'd be the right ones to give the cage to."

"I understand," Mom says.

"Desculpa, Mamã." I hope Mom forgets this soon. "You'll get a call from Mr. Lima next week. I'm sorry."

"I'll hear what he has to tell me."

"I miss Calvin," I say.

"I know," Mom says. "We found Calvin lifeless in the cage. We wanted to spare you. But we were wrong, and we're sorry. He deserved a funeral. He deserves all four of us to thank him for being part of this family. For loving us and letting us love him."

"Where is he?"

"Under the sugar apple tree," Mom says. A million butterflies fly from my tummy to my chest. "Do you want us to get another pet? Another chinchilla?"

"No," I say. "I need time. Let me think about it."

"You take all the time in the world you need," Mom says. "Until then, we can keep Calvin's cage in your room. It's a bit tight, but we can leave it here until you figure out what you want to do with it."

"Can you get me your marker with permanent ink?" I ask. "The one that writes and stays forever?"

"Amelia, what are you thinking?"

"Mamã, trust me," I say. "I'm ten."

Mom goes downstairs and brings me her black marker.

"Can you help me take the bars off the cage?"

Mom examines me with suspicious eyes, but her forehead is still a vast ocean, calm on a no-wind day. She's not trying hard to keep it still.

She helps me take the bars off.

"You can go," I say. "Por favor, Mamã. Trust me."

Mom leaves the room and takes slow steps downstairs. Once I stop hearing her footsteps on the wooden floor, I grab the marker. I lean over the cage's floor, white and clean as if no one ever lived there. I take a deep breath and write:

"To my friend Calvin, who's been with me forever. I learned from you that talking things out brings peace to my heart. I learned from you that dark things become brighter when I share them. You'll never need a cage to return to me because you'll always be in my heart. I'm forever your home. Love, Amelia."

I read my words over and over again. I don't want to write them wrong. I want everyone to know that Calvin lived here. This was his home for twenty-one years. We shared ten years together, and I'll never forget him.

I try to put the bars back into the cage's floor. They aren't right, but I'm sure Mom will help me fit them back in when she can.

I take the drawings I made for Calvin out of the cage. I store them in my desk drawer, next to the envelope with Calvin's picture and the paper note from Mom, Dad, and Lucas.

I take the two pieces that form Lucas's magic wand from under my bed. I try to put them together.

I can fit them perfectly together and wrap them with tape. I use a ton to make sure it doesn't fall apart.

I take the small twig out of my backpack. It's perfect as it is.

I leave the room and go downstairs to the kitchen. I take a sneak peek into Dad's office. It feels empty and weird, and I don't want to go inside. I go through the kitchen into the living room. Mom's warming her back next to a heater.

"Mamã," I say. "Call the pet clinic. You can give the cage to them."

"Are you sure?"

"Sure, sure," I say. "Lucas, I have to tell you something."

Lucas is glued to the television and hears nothing but the sound of the cartoons.

"Lucas!" I repeat.

"Hey!" Lucas complains as Mom shuts off the TV.

"The television is less important than any person in this house," Mom says. "You know that, Lucas. And your sister is talking to you."

Lucas shows me his laser-spewing eyes before I tell him what I did. This is not going well. Also, Mom keeps her full attention on us, which never works.

"Lucas, hmm." I don't know how to start this conversation. "I broke your magic wand." I better say it fast.

"What?" Lucas's mouth is open, and his eyes are already wet as he kneels on the floor.

"But I fixed it." I show him the wand. "See?"

Lucas cries his lungs out, and I don't know what to do. Mom stays out of our conversation, giving us space.

"You didn't fix it," Lucas shouts. "It's ruined."

"I know." I get close to Lucas. "I'm sorry. I didn't do it on purpose and did my best to fix it." I lean on my knees to be as close as I can to him. "It isn't great, I know. That's why I got you a new one. See?"

My hand goes into my back underneath my sweater. It comes back with the sugar apple small twig, the edges perfectly colored in a naturally lighter tone.

Lucas's eyes shine like two bright stars.

"It's not the same," Lucas says. "But I'll take it." He waits a few seconds and lowers his voice. "Obigado," Lucas thanks me, forgetting the "r" as he frequently does.

I smile and hug Lucas. He hugs me back.

Chapter 25

As long as there's love, there's hope. That's why I hoped for Calvin. I always will.

I believe Calvin lives in my heart. And he comes to mind whenever I see a sugar apple.

It's getting late, but there's still light outside.

I open the door and go down the steps into our backyard. In the corner next to the neighbor's wall lives our sugar apple tree.

I stand under it and glance above, working hard to see the sugar apples in the dim light. I spot one in the shape of a heart.

I take a deep breath and smell nothing. Sugar apples have no smell, but inside they're sweet and take time to be savored, like my Calvin.

I jump with my arm stretched into the air. My hand's high, and my fingers are open. They close as I feel a sugar apple leaf touching them, and my feet touch the ground, knees softly bent to support the fall.

I open my hand. It's empty.

I jump again and again. The branches are high for me, despite my three extra inches this year.

I get close to the trunk and touch it with both hands. My arms are straight against the wood. I lean to increase my strength and shake the trunk as hard as possible. It doesn't work. Not a single leaf falls to the ground.

I stand under the tree, watching the leaves and the branches like we're defying each other.

"Por favor," I say. "Just this time. Please."

The sugar apple tree stands tall and proud, higher than any tree in our backyard.

The lost flamingo crosses the sky over our house. It should be with the flock by now. Or maybe it's not the one I saw at school.

A rush of wind blows strongly with the flamingo's flight, smelling like seaweed and saltwater.

I cover my face with my hands only to see that leaves spread everywhere as I uncover it. Sugar apple leaves—soft, long, dark-green, and perfect.

I pick the leaves I need and place them under the tree, close to its trunk.

Bent over on my knees, my eyes look up. The sky is dark blue and orange. Clouds travel through the sky, and a light on the horizon gets smaller as the streetlights gain life.

"Obrigada," I say, "for bringing us together. Calvin and I."

I walk the yard searching for a sharp stone. I can't see much now, so I have to turn the outside lights on. I find a rock in the flower bed under the raspberry bush, close to the mudroom.

I run to the sugar apple tree, bend down on my knees again, and work my way around its trunk, close to the leaves I carefully put on the ground.

When I'm done, I take a few steps behind.

I stare at the tree and my work. My hands fall to the sides of my body, relaxed, the stone still in my right hand.

I switch the stone to my left hand and put it in my pocket.

I decide to keep it. It may come in handy.

I work the hair out of my face with my right hand and breathe in the smell of the orange blossom.

I pick up small white flowers covering the grass like a snow blanket. I place them on the floor, next to the leaves.

The air stands still. I can't feel a single breeze, which is rare here.

I take the stairs up inside the house, climbing two steps at once.

I open the door, close it behind me, and lean against it. There's no silence, and I can't hear the small cracks and snaps that remind me of Calvin—and always will.

Lucas is watching TV. Again. Dad's in the kitchen while Mom is talking to him from the living room, her back still close to the heater.

I hear Dad and Mom talking, and I watch Lucas on the couch, before he heads to the floor with his feet up against the backrest.

I clear my throat to get everyone's attention. It's too quiet, though, and no one stops to hear me.

I clear my throat again, this time louder.

"Hey," I shout.

"Hey!" Lucas immediately complains about the extra noise. He can't listen to his favorite cartoons.

"What?" Mom says. Her forehead starts to wrinkle, anticipating whatever problem between Lucas and me will arise.

"Amelia is making too much noise," Lucas says.

"I'm not," I say. "The TV is too loud, and no one listens to me."

"It's loud because you all make too much noise," Lucas says.

"Stop," Dad says. "What is it, Amelia?"

"Can you come outside?"

"Now?" Dad asks.

"Can it wait for tomorrow?" Mom asks. "We're getting dinner ready."

Well, Dad is getting dinner ready. And Lucas is only lying lazily on the couch. At least, that's what I see.

"No," I say. "You have to come now."

"Me?" Mom asks.

"All of you," I say. "Por favor," I beg.

"I'm not going," Lucas says.

"It's important," I say. "I think you'll like it." I stare at Lucas for him to understand that I'm specifically talking to him.

"Okay," Mom says. She eyes Dad. "Can you stop that for a minute?" And she watches me. "Is it going to take too long, Amelia?"

"Não," I promise, my hands together like I'm praying to show them that I mean it. Even ten-year-old grown girls have to use some tricks to have it their way.

"Let's go," Mom says. "You, too, Lucas."

Lucas blows out air to show us all he's not glad about this.

"Faster," Mom says.

Mom and time. She needs to get things going faster than everyone else.

Dad comes, too, and they all get their Crocs on.

I open the door and the night chill enters the living room and our clothes. It feels good on the cheeks.

Dad switches the rest of the outside lights on so no one stumbles down the steps.

"Here," I say and take them under the sugar apple tree.

In front of us, we can see the name *Calvin* written with sugar apple leaves sprinkled with tiny, white orange tree flowers.

I wrote Calvin's name and today's date on the tree trunk. Below the date, I marked the number twenty-one. Writing all this with a stone wasn't easy, but it came out well.

The four of us—Mom, Dad, Lucas, and I—stand in silence.

"Is this where Calvin is?" I ask.

"This is where he is," Mom says.

Dad nods in silence.

"Now," I continue, "I'd like us to hold hands and say a few words for him. Can we do that?"

"Obrigada," Mom starts. "For being part of this family, Calvin." She has no time to lose.

"Wait," I say. "Let's start by taking hands."

We form a circle, hand in hand.

"Thank you for being part of this family, Calvin," Mom repeats. "You brought us nothing but love." Mom smiles.

"You made me laugh," Lucas says. "I miss feeding you and watching you take a bath."

"We'll miss you," Dad says. Dad's a man of few words.

"Obrigada," I say. "For being my friend. Thank you for listening. I miss you. My heart is still sad, but I'll be okay. As long as you're okay, too. Goodbye, Calvin! Adeus."

We stay in a circle, smiling at each other, and I hope I remember this moment forever.

Dad, Mom, Lucas, and I release hands. Dad and Lucas turn to climb the stairs and go inside.

Mom stays a minute longer.

"You did a lovely job, Amelia," Mom says. "It was the most beautiful funeral. Calvin is lucky to have you as a friend."

"I had help." I smile, thinking of the sugar apple tree.

Mom scrunches her face in disbelief but adds nothing. She goes upstairs to the living room. She must be cold.

"You're coming?" Mom asks, turning back to peek at me before entering.

"Give me a sec," I say.

I keep staring at the tree and the leaves displayed on the floor.

A strong breeze comes when I turn my back to leave, and a deep shadow covers me from above, despite the dark sky.

I crouch in fear.

Staring up, I see the lost flamingo flying right over my head. It comes so close that the tiny flowers and the leaves forming Calvin's name dance in the air and fall on the floor like they mean nothing. It takes two more rounds in the air until it flies high and disappears into the night.

The breeze from the wings vanishes as fast as it comes. It made the funeral seem like nothing, but no breeze will erase Calvin's name on the tree trunk.

I stand under the branches, the hanging leaves, and the sugar apples.

"Obrigada," I say, breathing fast from the scare.

I imagine the tree bending to thank me back in the night.

"I couldn't do this on my own," I say, using low, inaudible words. "Thank you for helping me understand my feelings and to embrace and accept them. Thank you for helping me change. I wasn't ready. I'm more ready now."

I turn my back to the tree and run inside. My heart hurts as I twist the door handle, as if Calvin is twisting my heart's door handle to go inside. I hold my hand to my chest to ease the pain.

A grunt falls from the sky, and the flamingo crosses above me one last time. The pain increases and doesn't leave me, but I stand tall and get in.

I accept the pain in my chest as it is, and I know what it is: saudade. It comes with another thing I need to live: love.

Author's Note

A real long-tailed chinchilla inspired this fictional story. The chinchilla's name was Calvin, after the comic strip *Calvin and Hobbes,* by Bill Watterson. We shared our home and love with Calvin for the twenty-one years he lived with us.

Twenty-one years may seem like a lot. In the wild, chinchillas can live up to ten years. But if they live with humans caring for and loving them, they can last up to twenty years. Calvin proved precisely that.

Two species of chinchillas live today: *Chinchillas lanigera* and *Chinchilla chinchilla. Chinchillas lanigera* live in captivity as people's pets. They have long tails. They resemble a cross between a mouse, a rabbit, and a squirrel. They are more closely related to porcupines and guinea pigs despite their looks, though.

As a long-tailed chinchilla, Calvin was a small rodent with a large head, ears, and eyes. His forelimbs were much smaller and less developed than his hind limbs. He moved on all fours but also had fun hopping with his hind limbs. He had gray fur, which turned white on his tummy. He found different ways to get noticed and to keep us company, like growling and chattering his teeth.

The second species, *Chinchilla chinchilla,* are short-tailed chinchillas. They have shorter tails, smaller ears, and thicker necks than the *lanigera.*

Chinchillas arrived in the United States of America in 1923, long before landing in Europe. Mathias F. Chapman had a special license to import them, and he brought eleven. Nowadays, chinchilla pets in the US are descendants of these first eleven rodents.

When we welcomed Calvin to our home, I knew nothing about rodents or their social nature. I thought an animal living behind bars wouldn't socialize as much as other pets. I was wrong.

Calvin lived inside his cage. But we enjoyed freeing him in limited and safe areas. It was our way of sharing a common space and allowing him to be close to us.

We had to be vigilant, though. Calvin loved nibbling on the baseboards of our house, but he never bit any of us or any person introduced to him by us. He recognized our smell as a safe interaction.

Calvin enjoyed quiet, especially during the day. He squeaked to complain about too much hand movement inside his cage. He also squeaked for us to be aware of his presence.

It's true, and I told it in the story, that Calvin often fell, mostly when trying to jump bigger distances than he could handle, or while he was asleep, when he lost balance. When Calvin fell, he quickly recovered and returned to a comfortable position. Don't worry. He never got hurt from falling.

It's also true that Calvin provided us with a nonjudgmental ear. And besides our daily noises, he loved hearing music.

Humans and chinchillas have that in common—hearing ability and similar sensitivity to the same sound frequencies.

Calvin was aware of what was going on around him. That's one of the reasons why Amelia, in this story, loves talking to him more than anything else. The other reason is that everyone needs a friend to talk to. It can be a parent or another trusted adult, or even a pet.

We realized how much Calvin had been a part of our house when we lost him. We remember the noises, the smells, or him watching us when we approached.

After Calvin died, we decided to give his cage and accessories away to a pet clinic. We kept a clothespin that we used in his cage.

The gnawed clothespin is not a beautiful object. Still, it symbolizes Calvin's presence.

We framed the clothespin and hung it above the space once occupied by Calvin's cage. It was our way of honoring his memory.

I believe that small things and memories ground us. They give us the foundation to overcome any challenges ahead.

My experience with Calvin taught me that love connects us to all living beings. It also showed me that loving implies letting go when the right moment comes. It's a challenging experience when we spend a quarter of our life together.

After Calvin, we decided not to own another chinchilla. The main reason for that decision was that we felt that wild animals belong in nature. But be aware that keeping a pet chinchilla is not a bad thing. Chinchillas sold at the pet store are not captured from the wild but are captive-bred. Owning a chinchilla actually means helping an endangered species.

Wild chinchillas live in the Andes Mountains of northern Chile in South America. They used to live in Peru,

Argentina, and Bolivia, but now they seem to be extinct in these areas.

The International Union for Conservation of Nature (IUCN; https://www.iucn.org/pt) gathers government and civil society organizations. They gather data to measure the status of conservation needs and efforts in the natural world.

The IUCN Red List of Threatened Species (https://www.iucnredlist.org/) works as a "barometer of life." That means it assesses the global extinction risk status of animal, fungus, and plant species. And it currently lists the long-tailed chinchilla as endangered. The wild adult population continues to decrease.

Natural predators, like birds of prey, foxes, and other small carnivorous animals, capture chinchillas to survive. But human activity has decimated the wild chinchilla population for reasons beyond survival. This activity includes poaching, mining, and agriculture.

Still, the main reason why chinchillas are at risk is because of their prized fur. Humans love to wear chinchilla fur. It is soft and dense and represents distinctiveness and status.

Chinchillas have about fifty to sixty hairs per follicle, but they need their thick fur to survive the harsh weather at high elevations. Chinchillas are also most active during the night—when the temperatures fall to cold extremes.

Our skin would need to adapt if we faced the same conditions. But we don't. And that's why we humans have only one to three hairs per follicle. We don't need to wear chinchilla fur.

Government regulations protecting chinchillas triggered the fur industry to provide new directions. The industry decided that the fur used in coats must come from farm (not wild) chinchillas. This change reduced the risk of poaching.

It breaks my heart to know that wild chinchillas are still at risk, but being sad provides no help. We need to take action.

One way to be active is by volunteering to help. Search for nonprofit organizations like Save the Wild Chinchillas (https://www.savethewildchinchillas.org/).

You can also contact local authorities and search for local organizations to aid conservation efforts. Ask your parents or another adult you trust for help to get involved.

About the Author

Inês F. Oliveira lives in Portugal in a small city by the sea with her husband and two children. She holds a master's degree from Carnegie Mellon University and has committed many years to the technological field. That was before turning to words and writing. She finds the best stories to tell in the small things and can't stop admiring the world through her children's eyes.